Also by Norman Fruchter: *Coat Upon a Stick*

single file

single file

Norman Fruchter

alfred a. knopf
new york
1970

This is a Borzoi Book
Published by Alfred A. Knopf, Inc.

Copyright © 1970 by Norman Fruchter

All rights reserved under International and Pan-American Copyright Conventions.
Published in the United States by Alfred A. Knopf, Inc., New York,
and simultaneously in Canada by Random House of Canada Limited, Toronto.
Distributed by Random House, Inc., New York.

Library of Congress Catalog Card Number: 74–106626

Manufactured in the United States of America

First Edition

single file

6 am-10 am
april 7, 1965
The —— Hospital is an average New York City public building; designed by an engineer, built for three times as much as it should have cost, resembling a prison. Inside it looks like a hospital, late Victorian model; arched, tunnel-like corridors, institutional green paint, a pox on all decoration. NO SMOKING! Smells? Chlorine, Lysol, and antiseptics assault and wrinkle your nostrils everywhere except in the Out-Patients' waiting room, where congealed sweat, rotting teeth, an accumulation of farts and the exudes of domestic diseases conquer all disinfectants.

INTERNS' JOKE
Preventive health kills slower.

You can distinguish the sick from their relatives and friends because the sick exhale. They stare, unfocused, slack-jawed, or they drift through uneasy sleep, occasionally snoring. They heat the dim, vaulted ceiling with their soaring fevers, from pneumonias and tuberculoses, familiar and unclassifiable viruses, abscesses ranging out of control through already defenseless tissue. And into that air, vibrating with temperatures, others contribute the odors of attrition from corrosive ulcers, raw piles, eroded livers, and the cancers of indulgence and reproduction. The —— Hospital never begins its student nurses in Out-Patients, preferring the relative tranquillity of Maternity Ward for initiation, but sooner or later every trainee is transferred to this grim frontier where penurious and punitive public medicine fights a daily delaying action against the city's diseases. A few trainees gag at the smells, and an even smaller number cry at the predictable pathos of individual cases, in spite of the warnings issued during Orientation Week about the irrelevance of compassion to effective nursing.

3

Mostly they knew the score long before they wriggled into
their stiff white uniforms, blacks and Puerto Ricans and the
last remnants of the shanty Irish, nobody else needs such an
ambiguous profession these days. After two or three weeks the
smell penetrates, a familiar, through starched white cloth and
scrubbed layers of young skin. Eyes no longer hesitate and
blink, momentarily hooded by drooping lashes, but slip
quickly, though accurately, given the standards taught, over
each stooped figure waiting at the examining desk. "Figuroa.
Your first name's Raimondo? You spell that with a y or an i?"

*Not so many forms now, they've been simplified, and you need an
address for the case's sake, suppose he has to go home in an
ambulance? And you have to be strict with them, otherwise they'll
talk your ear off, half of them aren't really sick they don't have
anybody to talk to. But we don't have time to play social worker,
not with a full waiting room every day.*

After six months' training, an eighteen-year-old slips into
more than her uniform.

NEIGHBORHOOD   The —— nurses are the hottest. They'll screw anywhere, taxis or
LEGEND   telephone booths. The doctors lay them right on their desks, or in
the operating theaters whenever there's a table free. And I heard
one patient got himself some pussy right in the ward toilet!

Matto waited four and a half hours.

Never mind how early he woke, no connection between what
jerked him out of sleep twenty minutes past dawn and the

dreams he drifted into, slumped, cross-legged, on the
slatted benches engraved with three generations of uncertain
carvings.

*Puppet show. Web of wires into skeleton of fish, bony fish arrow,
eyehole and quivering tail. THIS WAY. Unwillingly he tiptoes, the
message was important, he must speak clearly. "It's not a carp.
For sure. The only good carp was on Balzano's boats."*

Wet white bones, glistening like licked fingernails. Tooth-
white. Fleshy hunks that evaded Negrone's knife, clung
stubbornly to white bone. Tougher than chicken bone, sharp
enough to cut and sting—cross-hatchings of scars creased
Negrone's wrist up to his elbow, a foot above the cuff of his
rubber gloves. Carp skeletons stacked, moist rattles, in
Negrone's brine-soaked buckets.

"Why you use wood, Gerry?" Grunting under its weight as he
braced, flat-footed, on the swaying deck and shifted the barrel
across the foot of dirty water between bow and dock.
Negrone, balding and thin, nervous hands whicking the knife
edge clean of scales before starting another carp, flicked a
spatter of slime across the boards to Matto's feet.

"Metal would be worse, time we're finished a run. These
buckets, sure they soak up water but they drain it, too.
Anything else I use, even the new rubber ones they're making,
they'd start out light but they'd break your back by the time
they're full. Besides the fillets wouldn't drain, I'd still hafta
dry them on newspaper after we unloaded, otherwise the
market wouldn't take them. Half their weight is water.
Wood"—his ring hand slapped the side of the barrel—"wood's

5

old-fashioned, people think, but it's still better than anything else."

Took Matto seven months of working the day-labor agencies after Scarduzzio laid him off the DPW road gang to remember Gus Balzano. Not that he forgot, only three years since Luzon and the QM outfit Balzano ran as an adjunct to his major business, liquor supplier for three infantry regiments. Balzano took Matto on as soon as he saw him, without waiting for Matto to stammer the name of the town his Aunt Carrie always said his mother came from. (Nobody knew where his father was raised.) "We're in this together, old buddy, we'll get a little back for what they do to the old country." They got a little back. Matto lost over $5,700 on a converted refrigerator ship that took twenty-five days from Okinawa to San Francisco. (*Losers' joke by the eighteenth day:* When the captain breaks even, we'll raise anchor.) Seven months of pocketing sixty cents an hour, after commission, loading rented trucks ten hours a day before he finally decided to find Balzano and ask for help. Any kind of help. Angie remembers they spread an Esso map across Tony's counter, tried to show him with red crayon the routes south through the tunnel and the Jersey flatlands to Baltimore; he couldn't even read the numbers. He dodged cops on Fremont Avenue for two weeks before somebody in a bar who'd heard of Balzano sent him across the bay to the Eastern Shore; another three days, stiff-jointed from nights wrapped in soggy deck canvas on untended boats, before he found Balzano and mumbled his apologies. His face burned throughout Balzano's back-slapping reminiscences, finally he slunk away with the two tens Balzano peeled off to buy himself some white ducks and

6

the black and white striped boat-neck jerseys worn by all the sailors on Balzano's boats.

Matto was initiated as a deck hand. After a summer of service, Balzano promised to apprentice him to Negrone ("fastest fish stripper on the Chesapeake"), the thin, mournful Milanese who supervised the trimming, cleaning, and stacking of the fillets and carted the winy water-soaked barrels of carp to market every Sunday evening, using two trucks Balzano borrowed from his cousin who borrowed them from the trucking fleet of a wholesale fish dealer, open Monday through Friday. The operation was a race against market deadlines, with hazards like slow leaks in old tires, boiling radiators, and busted generators to increase the odds, speedometers doctored and gas tanks refilled so carefully that for five years the fish dealer never discovered that some of the carp his drivers brought back from market Monday morning had arrived at the market in his own trucks just three hours before.

But deck hands were both swabbies and stewards in Balzano's navy. Technicians like Negrone could work below decks, shielded from the admiring squeals of Eastern Shore women who jabbed unsheathed fingernails into Matto's biceps as he hauled up their lines, heavy with a wriggling strike on fat bait—Balzano never stinted. They lost their breakfast and lunch and dinner in the calmest seas, blew their rotten-cheese breath into Matto's face as he eased them down polished ladders to their carefully fitted bunks. Balzano kept the liquor flowing, supplied by another cousin straight from the harbor, partially smashed crates, 40 per cent reduction. By Saturday afternoon the parties were usually looped, especially the college girls Balzano preferred, homegrown, honey-blonde, Sweet-

briar, Randolph-Macon, even the U of V where he sent
Bianca. ("Goddammit if she don't keep her legs closed till after
she's married I swear to God I'll break her head.") Matto
never trusted himself to answer their questions, slid awkwardly
past young flesh advertising itself in brief bathing suits that
rarely braved water and lowered his buckets of carp to
Negrone's cutting table.

*Camilla slashed her wrists this morning. Carson took the
phone message from Bellevue and left the SSE clearance on
my desk; she was waiting for me when I barged into her office.
"Now just don't holler that you told me so or I'll transfer you
right out of this section. I reread her whole file this morning,
I knew I'd have plenty of time before you showed up. You did
what you could for that family, you even tried to get
Supplementary so Camilla could move out. And what's more,
I initialed every goddam one of your emergency requests
and your furniture grants. I even sent that goddam
Supplementary up to Schwartzchild in Divisional,
after I swore I'd never ask that sonofabitch for another favor.
And I ordered you to lay off, remember? You been here
too long to indulge yourself."*

*Carson really works at playing supervisor. Every time she
puts me down for indulgence I feel like kicking her discolored
teeth in. Gold fillings and nicotine stains, two packs a day
since she made supervisor, she seems to have acquired white
nerves. But when I got back to my desk and leafed through my
notebook, I was able to think about Camilla rather than
my complicity. Was that a gain? Should Carson be compli-
mented? I reread my notes.*

9/18/64
Mr. Torres laid off from NY Central. How long ago did
UIB finish? Check with state. Register him for DER.
Camilla's job—Refined Hosiery, 221 West 35th. Packer at
$50/week. Laid off—doesn't remember date, says it was a
seasonal slowdown. And giggles. Check employer—
Pincus, AL7–3125.

9

9/21/64

Worker in living room of Torres family. Also present:
Mrs. Torres, Camilla, Mrs. Ortiz, Mr. Rivera, the two
younger children, Alfredo and Dolores, and Mrs. Ortiz's
youngest daughter, Teresa Vasquez, who was visiting.
Worker asked if Victor was home and Camilla went into
the back bedroom and told him to get out of bed. (Worker
did not request that this be done.) Mrs. Ortiz's daughter
Teresa did most of the translating.

*I sat stiffly in their one guest armchair, covered with clear
plastic which the occasional heat from the steam riser cracked
and split when the kids shoved it too close. Usually I grinned
a lot, the more people crowded around me the broader I
grinned. Sometimes I cracked my knuckles, sometimes I
alternated grinning with a probing lick of both corners of my
mouth. At all times I tried to remember to look concerned
and helpful.*

re Mrs. Ortiz:

Mrs. Torres suggested to the worker that her mother,
Mrs. Ortiz, might be better off in a nursing home because
she's too old to take care of herself, not sufficiently
ambulatory to attend the clinic by herself, not able to be
properly taken care of by anyone else in the household.
As far as the worker could ascertain, Mrs. Ortiz seemed to
agree with this evaluation. She exhibited no fears about
the possibility of entering a nursing home, but in general
her thought processes seem scattered and she seems unable to
concentrate clearly on her immediate situation. (Check
on Geriatrics referral.)

re Victor:

Mrs. Torres said a Youth Board worker whose name she

10

forgot (check with LES YB Hdqrs) had already spoken to Victor, and he's agreed to go back to school. YB worker will handle all necessary reregistrations. Victor seemed pleased with this arrangement.

Translation: Victor didn't seem displeased, at least as far as I could tell, since he never got out of bed. And Mrs. Torres actually said she couldn't remember the Youth Board worker's name because "so many social workers walk in and out of here every week, I think sometimes they come just to see each other. If I charged admission I would make more money than I get off the Welfare."

re Mr. Rivera:
His UIB expired in '63. Told worker he's been mostly out of work for a year and a half." Not contributed anything substantial to the family for the past six months. Camilla, Alfredo, and Dolores are *his* children, living with Mrs. Torres but not accountable on her budget. Mr. Rivera said he is willing to go off the Welfare but wants his children taken care of. Worker explained that as long as he lives in the Torres household he and his children must have a separate category. Worker asked him why he was living in the Torres household part of the time and with another woman the rest of the time. He shrugged his shoulders. Worker asked him whether the other woman was the mother of Camilla, Alfredo, and Dolores and he shook his head. Worker asked him how he got along with Mrs. Torres and he smiled. Mr. Rivera is perhaps fifty-five, squat and powerfully built in spite of his illness, and his face, creased and scarred, shows his years. Worker would have found it hard enough asking him these questions directly, let alone through the medium of translation.

11

Once in Mrs. Hayes's kitchen I asked Curtis, in a joking
manner I thought and with no offense I could recognize
except perhaps envy, how he managed so many women. "How
come it's your business how I get my ass?" he snapped.
"Does anybody ask you how you spend your nights?" "But
he ain't on the State," Mrs. Hayes snorted. "Me neither,"
Curtis said.

9/27/64
Worker met Camilla at a luncheonette, bought her pie and
coffee (see expense record attached). "I can't say anything
about how I really feel in front of them. In front of him."
Speaks surprisingly good English. Says she can't stand
Mr. Rivera (her stepfather) and is afraid he'll begin making
advances to her again. Says she would give anything to move
out. "Any place would be better than living with him."

We sat at a cramped table way in the back of Barney's,
I picked a Jewish place so nobody would see her talking to
me and spread the word back to Mr. Rivera. Moe the
counterman gave her the cold shoulder till I finally caught up
with her by the ice-cream freezer; then he rewarded me with
a leer, a nod, and a poke in the ribs. I wiped his crummy table
with somebody's leftover napkin, uncertain crescent of lipstick
smudge amazed me, do women still blot their lips? Her own
lipstick was sparse and nicely applied, and anyway she didn't
need it. I brushed some crumbs off my lap, grazed an
unprofessional erection with my knuckles. She was busty
with good loose-swiveling hips, wore her blouse too many
buttons open. I concentrated on my coffee.

"You don't know him. Ever since he's out of work, drunk all

the time, calling my mother filthy names. His hands are all over the house."

She sneered, twisting her upper lip into more distaste than I can reproduce, and brushed at the hem of her pleated skirt. I pitied them both. I could sense the flow of her liquids, he was into his dry season. "Where'd he get the money? To get drunk on?"

She shrugged, less than contempt, fluid twist of her right shoulder. "Somewhere. I don't know. Momma wouldn't give him any." And bitterly. "Don't worry, it didn't come out of the budget!"

I bought her another cup of coffee and waited till she cooled down. We talked about what she could do, the business schools and the nursing programs that might admit her, the jobs that were always available. "What I like is all the great choices I have," she said, sourly. "Suppose all this stuff falls through, what can you do to help me get a place of my own?" Not much, I told her, and that, at least, was accurate enough. "Thanks heaps," she said. "I'll try," I said, and after all, Carson would say, she didn't actually manage to kill herself, just scarred her wrists.

The SSE turned out to be a notification that Mr. Sung was dead. My guess is they found him by the river, too early in the morning for anybody but the precinct cruisers, who thought he was asleep. Took me three months to finally corner Mr. Sung, and then I was ashamed of the hackneyed nature of my responses. "Oho, so we finally meet, Mr. Sung," I crowed,

*flickers of old Charlie Chan movies. He nodded me to his
one kitchen chair; I caught myself just before I bowed him
thank-you. It wasn't his fault my records showed he hadn't
received a Statutory Visit for more than two years. Perhaps
my predecessors, those faceless fillers of volumes of forms
whose assaults on language affront me less than my own, had
understood Mr. Sung's practice; bare room that smelled of
scalding tea-kettle water dousing already spotless surfaces.
Once he'd worked in a laundry and before that in a restaurant.
His past was inviolate. Would DW ever hire specialists to
ascertain which categories of rage and embarrassment he shields
behind those exquisite manners? I perched on the edge of his
substantial chair, certain my weight would collapse it, aware
of every shred of mud I'd tracked into his spotless cell on the
soles of my canvas shoes. To cover myself I stare at his walls
and decide he needs new wallpaper, he says that in the spring
he hopes to be able to paint. I tell him there are grants available and besides, renovations are the landlord's responsibility.
He thanks me gravely, have I imparted information or noise?
At least I know enough not to ask about his children.*

re Mr. Sung:
Same room for the last five years. No furniture except a
single mattress, electric hot plate, small kitchen table, and the
chair from which worker conducted interview. Worker
pointed out grants were available for additional furniture—
offer graciously refused. Worker inspected rent receipts
dated 1/15 to 3/30. Mr. Sung said his health was excellent
and that he was managing well on his checks. He said he
likes living in his room and that he often walks from the
hotel to the square. #661 issued for $50.85—one suit and
one pair of shoes.

14

Perhaps you need a new suit, Mr. Sung? Record summer
coming, very hot in the square, you sweat with heavy jacket.
Any hole or sign of wear on his soles would justify a new pair
of shoes. Please lift your feet, Mr. Sung? An impossible
request. How are your shoes holding out? Oh very fine, very
fine, I could hear him nod his answer. I spoke finally so that
I'd stop watching his tiny boneless hands. "Mr. Sung, pardon
me for asking, but what do you do with your time? Besides
walking to the square and reading your Chinese newspaper?"
Which was neatly folded beside his teapot.

For an instant his eyes confront me, tiny, milky whites.
Somewhere a shutter opens. "Every morning, when sun comes
up, I walk to the river."

Pending: HALLORHAN, Warren James
Collateral—saw Mrs. Higgins, landlady—says he owes from
the middle of March. Then found him in his room. Watching
television. Son-in-law gave it to him for Xmas, cheap set,
thinks it costs about $60. Forgot to get the make or model
number. Worker asked him why his son-in-law couldn't
help him out with the rent and food instead of giving him
TV. Client responded that it was a Xmas gift and not help,
they couldn't afford to help, they had four children of their
own. Promised either to return set or else sell it and transfer
money to DW.

We both stared at the TV after he shouted for me to come in.
Kids' cartoons the only stuff on in the afternoons, we both
stared at an enormous stupid worm, stovepipe hat and a
lipstick grin. "I know, I know, I'm not allowed to have a
TV." I put my book on his radiator and made a big show of

15

*tying my laces. "Forget it," I said, "I didn't see it." I can't
stand when their eyes beg, my hundred and ten bucks a week
doesn't buy that much power. "Or if I saw it, it was a gift,
a Christmas present. You couldn't help it, you've been trying
to get rid of it for months. You know the rules, for Chrissake,
better than I do, you won't get caught for chiseling. Now
close your mouth and sit down and stop worrying about it,
you make me nervous scraping the floor."*

Scheduled to report to UIB on 4/15. Misplaced last check
stub but says he received 3/27 allotment. Claims he paid
rent till 4/3—check with landlady again. Claims he received
no check for period ending 4/5. Was intending to visit DW
center "in a day or two."

re specific problem—last time he visited AA was in January,
basement of a church in Brooklyn, says he doesn't like to go
where he might be known. Told him of various complaints
entered against him, also agency reports (see accompanying
file). Says he's been "basically dry" since last Thanksgiving.

*"I've been looking for work, sure I've been looking, but it's
no use. As soon as I show up, they start to snicker. And not
behind my back, either. 'You got any dishwashing jobs for an
old rummy?' one of them smart-ass Spics hollered at me,
I wanted to spit in his face but he's a state employee, right,
if he reported me it'd show up in your records. And I can't
take no chances with the Welfare, it's all I got."*

*When Laurie notices, she says I look less tentative. Carson
thinks I'm anemic and recommends vitamin pills. They can
both shove it.*

16

Not fear. The first few days, rediscovering his rhythms, he pitied Laurie her continuities, stretched himself to service her needs, carefully scrubbing off Angie's secretions. But his edginess won out. He felt the distance behind which he lurked, wary. Nerves in his neck jangled as Laurie's cool fingers teased a lock of his hair. "I should cut that. It's really too long in back."

"I don't need it cut. I like it long. Maybe I'll grow a beard again."

He watched her hesitate. "You're getting hardly any sleep at all." More than solicitous. "I hear you dragging up the stairs, you've got no energy left! You don't have to keep me out of it—I mean, whatever's draining you, we could try to talk about it."

He grunted, shifting on the rocker, aware of his drooping eyelids, stubbled skin taut over his cheekbones, grateful he didn't have to fake weariness. "Look, I can't talk about it." Despairing wave of hand which he let drop, limp, onto his thigh. "Besides, it's just the same old shit. Some weeks are worse than others, that's all. I faked a set of reports, except I couldn't get interested enough to make them credible. And I probably didn't fool Carson anyway, she'll decide where to draw the line. I've just had it, that's all. I should quit instead of waiting for Carson to haul me into her office."

Stared at his polished toe, why doesn't she notice I always manage to find the time to keep my boots shiny? He could feel her stare, commiserating, until her chair scraped and she tiptoed into the kitchen; from the sound of the tins he worked out she was brewing the Chinese tea she used only for special

17

occasions. "It's not that serious," he grinned as she set the tray next to him on the coffee table. "I'll manage." And accepted her quick kiss on his temple.

"I'll have to work late tonight. Harrison's still way behind but he's pushed *Playfair*'s deadline back so many times he's stuck now, we've got to deliver or else they'll scream bloody murder and he'll probably lose the next contract. If he hasn't already. But it's torture for him to spend more than an hour at the easel, he thinks I don't see the faces he makes when he turns away. He's got bottles and bottles of prescription pain-killers but they just dope him up so he can't work; his doctor says nothing can cure colitis but a total change of scene. Or else six months in the hospital. His breath's so terrible I fight to keep from turning my head away whenever he talks to me."

"That's okay. Maybe I'll try to get some work done, put some of those notes together. I can eat out." He cut her off as she started to reassure him that there was plenty of food.

It can't last, he thought, her heels clopping down the stone stairs, sooner or later I'll slip up. New nicotine stains on my nails and the ball of my index finger, smoking mornings in Angie's bed; when she asks I'll say I'm chain-smoking while I walk. Do I ever talk in my sleep, mumble a fragment of name or reach out to graze or nuzzle someone she'll recognize as other? I never felt capable of sustaining this complicated a deception before.

While Laurie worked he slept.

LAURIE   *I suppose Harrison thinks I'm wasting myself. Naturally he'll never say. But when he frowns sometimes as he thumbs through my*

18

sketches, and not in disapproval, he doesn't need to talk. I know my
hands. The first two years he kept waiting for me to quit, branch out
on my own, perhaps even go after some of his business. That night
after Tanya's party when we went to Lenny's and he got drunk,
he admitted he'd considered offering me a partnership. I laughed in
his face. "I don't want your stomach." And hoped he was drunk
enough to forget, he thinks I'm never bitchy. I knew how much pain
that liquor would cost him. And besides I've always had perfect
digestion, even if he leaves me I'll probably go on eating three meals
a day. Both of them think I'm a vacuum. "Why do I have to want
something out there, something that would label me? I like what
I do, isn't that enough? You and Harrison are so competitive you
can't imagine anyone could just let themselves be. You're both always
waiting for me to shift gears and become somebody. Emerge." But
now he doesn't push me any more, troubles himself only so's not to
disturb me. Is that what I wanted?

An hour after she left, her phone call woke him. Groped the
receiver toward his ear and mumbled back at her soft hello,
wanting to ask how long the phone'd been ringing before he
finally fumbled it off its cradle. "Were you asleep?"

He yawned, audibly, decided, his brain barely turning over,
that it was safe to admit it. "Yeah."

"I'm sorry I woke you." And with a rush: "Look, love, I don't
mean to spring this on you but Harrison's insisting that we go
up to his place and finish the stuff this weekend. I know it's
absolutely last minute, but Harrison swears he just can't take
another second in the office, he feels so sick it'll just be much
easier for him to take a half-hour nap if he's only ten steps
away from his bedroom. And the light in his studio's so much

19

nicer than the light in the office, since we have to work to-morrow and Sunday anyway. And Melanie's ecstatic with the thought of cooking for both of us, she says I won't have to lift a finger, you know how she loves to pamper."

Still numb. What else was she trying to apologize for?

More hesitant. "Don't be angry, love. I wouldn't have been worth much this weekend anyway, running up to the office every spare minute. And you don't have to worry about the shopping, either. I'll do it all Monday afternoon when I get home." And a pause. "It's just that we have to get this job finished and it'll be so much easier at Harrison's."

"Well," he said, furry tongue slow in a dry mouth. "One thing for sure, I envy you Melanie's cooking."

"Yes, I know." Rush of relief, at his yielding so quickly? What had she prepared for, a long mulish fight? These days? "I'm looking forward to it myself. Especially her fritters!"

"Don't eat too much. Watch yourself." Suddenly jovial, three nights of absolute freedom. "You're getting fat, you've got a real spread! You think I'm too sleepy to see that roll of flesh you pinch in the mirror after you snap your bra closed. You come back from Melanie's cooking with more than an extra pound or two on you and I'll kick your ass!" Swallow, hoping she wouldn't say, I wish you would.

"I am not getting fat!" Mock outrage only.

"Well, you ask Harrison. He ought to know. He sees you more than I do." He yawned again. "Look, try not to work too hard. That's a terrible pressure you're taking on, both of you been

20

knocking yourselves out this last stretch. Harrison'll put himself in the hospital if he keeps this up."

"Don't worry. At least this way we'll all get some rest. I left some chili in the icebox. It's in the brown bowl, cover it over with foil afterwards. And there's plenty of eggs. And hamburger meat in the freezer, you just have to defrost it." "Don't worry about me. I'll reassert my fading bachelor rights, get Marty and Ellen to feed me supper. Ellen still owes me money from that World Series bet, I'll take my payment in kind." Not the kind I'd prefer, but probably all I'll get. "In kindness. I'll just call up and claim my winnings. And Sunday night I'll get Harriet and Tim to take me uptown to that Indian place." Knowing she'd be pleased, occasionally worried at what pleasures her tastes denied him.

"I'd better go. Harrison is making desperately frothy passes at me from the drafting table." Breathless again. "We'll be done some time on Monday. We have to be. So I'll be home Monday afternoon at the latest." About to hang up, she was groping. "Maybe we can even go see a movie Monday night." He let her wait for an answer. "I'll miss you."

Bullshit. But he didn't even snort. Twitches of contempt and shame chased themselves down his spine. "I'll miss you. Kiss Melanie for me, but tell her I've still got bones to pick. Maybe another time I can manage not to lose my temper at her table. Goodbye." He guessed her brisk whirl to Harrison, elated, another successful maneuver to escape his office. But her image faded after her receiver clicked. He set the phone down and his apartment expanded before him, fresh, for an instant a stranger's home, artifact of unfamiliar taste. He stumbled, barefoot, into the living room, struck by its comfortable white severity—low, rough pine wall benches Laurie had insisted on broken by the wild pillow puffs she'd sewn and stuffed herself, rows of bookshelves he'd clumsily hung bearing wares that carefully defined a pair of sensibilities contemporary, if not catholic. "This is yours, you live here?" the little girl he'd picked up at *The Tattoo* had exclaimed. He realized what she'd seen.

LAURIE   *He waited a week to tell me about her, and then insisted it didn't mean anything. Which was much, much worse. But I let myself be persuaded.*

Rainy October in a fall she ruined for him, forcing arguments about her operation. "It doesn't make sense to postpone it any longer. My periods aren't getting any easier, and none of the doctors we saw had any hopes they would. If anything, they're getting more painful! And whenever we finally do decide to have a child, I'll have to get it done anyway, and the more I wait, the harder it'll be, recuperating. I'm not getting any younger. I want to have it done. I want it over with, once and for all." Glowered at her, sullen, incapable of discovering whatever logic might dissuade her. Knife-happy doctors convinced her, New York's a surgeon's paradise. "You don't know anything about it. You think you're brave, but even a headache knocks you out. This'll flatten you for months, it's not like tonsils, you don't walk out the next day with a sore throat. I know, I watched my uncle go through three operations, you'll feel like you're renting somebody else's body. For months afterwards you'll ache, you'll wake up with your scar throbbing or run short of breath coming home from the supermarket and

22

have to rest on somebody's stoop wondering if you'll ever get your energy back. Any operation upsets your equilibrium, and messing with tubes is not minor, no matter what those doctors said." He stared at the clenched line of her jaw as she shook her head. "You're wrong to try to protect me, this isn't another test I have to be convinced not to attempt. It's got to happen, you can't keep putting it off just because I take pain badly. You're only thinking about yourself, you're worried I'll be impossible to live with until I heal, you might even have to minister to me! I'll go to Sharon's till I'm well enough to fend for myself, for god's sake, the last thing I'd do is let something as minor as an operation interfere with your comfort. It's taken me two months to convince myself to go through something we knew was inevitable all along, why are you trying to stop me?"

No answer but moroseness. Sulk. She didn't instinctively hate all doctors, bloodsuckers and hypocrites, didn't feel debased by their cold hands and calculating grins, who should she trust? And in theory, of course, he was committed to the idea of children, once the time was clearly right. She wore him down by repeating herself, not the first time he'd lost a sustained argument and swore she'd pay. "It's not you who has to put up with the pain every month. Even the damn Darvon doesn't help that much—when I do conk out for a couple of hours I wake up feeling seasick. Or stoned."

"I have to put up with its effects, I never imagined it was pleasant! But we get through it. And there's other drugs you haven't tried yet! If you think the pain balances what you'll go through just on the chance that they can straighten it out,

23

then go ahead. But don't think it's just a week in the hospital. It's three months, four months out of your life, how the hell do you measure that one?"

"I'll find out," she said. She did. The nurses let him stay twenty minutes after visiting hours ended, until they produced the pill that would grant a fuddled but syrupy doze. "I'm afraid we must be going now, sir." He kissed Laurie goodbye, containing his rage till he reached the hallway and then stomped down the corridor, aching to arc fat gobs of phlegm over the thin white curtains of each ward doorway, fuck asepsis! They beat me, he kept whispering, they beat me good, expertise again. They made up their minds first time they saw her, another candidate, another guinea pig, and tomorrow morning they'll cut her. Fucking butchers! They'll wheel her in, knocked out, ashen, transfusions and intravenous ready on those goddam metal trees they hook to the bed, spinal she won't even feel paralyzing her, ready for dissection. Another lab animal! Bastards. Nursing his third whisky at *The Tattoo*'s bar he caught her eyes, masked by too much shadow under an elfin haircut, watching him in the huge mirror. Lifted his shotglass in what he hoped was wry salute and downed it, managing to swallow without grimacing. And held her stare, without winking back, till the liquor settled, then pivoted down off his stool and marched across to bow with a flourish intended as debonair. "If a girl like you knows what she's doing in a place like this, you'll come home with me. If you survey judiciously what's left of the clientele, I'm by far the best bet, given the hour and the possibilities." He bowed again, grinning until he realized how muddled it'd come out, afterwards he forgot to ask just what she'd heard. But he stood his ground

24

as she stared at him, neither evaluative nor hostile. Barely curious. He was certain he wasn't blushing. She was built pretty small. If she didn't decide soon, he wouldn't buy her the drink he'd intended. His credits ledgered, he yawned. "You just don't fit," she said, "I bet you never come here. I bet this is the first time you ever came here and now you're afraid you'll wake up. Poom!" She jabbed through an enormous balloon some two inches above his head, sucked air into a ghoulish pout as it deflated. Curiously long fingernails for such shaggy hair, he thought. "I'm not afraid. If you think you can wake me up why don't you try?" She turned to stare at him but he watched her eyes slip off. He waited till he was sure she'd forgotten, then tapped her knobby elbow. "I guess I'm not interested," she said. "I'm not selling anything. And certain people spend enough time telling me I don't have anything anybody wants." As she sucked her fingernail he wanted to urge her to bite it, clean. "Okay, I'll come. Promise you won't talk too much if I ask you not to. But on the other hand," and her tongue probed the scaly underside of her nail again, "promise me you'll talk all night if I want you to. Or at least put a record on. I've been getting confused lately. Well, come on," she said, he was still wondering about her drink. "Lead me the way out of here." Reached for her shoulder bag and slipped off her stool.

In the street he asked her name, amazed it was happening so easily. Jessie, for Jessica, which was, nowadays, old-fashioned. "Jessie's a boy's name too and that's why I like it!" And grinned up at him, thin lips and a tipped nose, quick wrinkle, warm throb in his tight crotch reminded him he'd forgotten to worry about how well he'd manage with her, clearly been around.

25

A genuine waif, and Laurie gone for a week. Possibilities? Which didn't emerge. "My first real night downtown, I only just split. Spade cat who fed me out of his own pocket, claimed it was the first time for him it wasn't the other way around. If I had any bread he coulda used it, that's not why he kicked me out. He kicked me out because they put him uptight, that's all. I told him I was colorblind and I showed him, too, all I could, but they just put him too uptight."

"I know the daytime side of that a little bit. I work for the Welfare. The State."

She whistled, then sucked on a loose strand of her shoulder strap as they walked south. "The man with the black book. I seen you all over, uptown. Nobody likes your goodies much."

"Nobody should."

Climbing his stairs he considered how to tell her about Laurie so she'd have to listen, curious about whatever judgment she'd make. But he forgot as soon as she dumped her coat on Laurie's stool. "Is all this really yours? It's really—and all these books? And you made the benches?" He didn't deny it. "And all those paintings?"

"Friends." Feeling by now it was almost a lie.

"All this. So much room. You can sit up here and rock for hours and nobody can get to you. Come here," she whispered, and after he crossed his room to sit before her on the rocker so she could cradle his head and lose her small fingers in his tangled hair, she rocked and rocked and matched the rhythms of her talk to the chair's creak. "I never stayed with anybody who had a home before, never. Can you imagine that? My

26

stepdaddy kicked me out of Grand Rapids, Michigan, when I was fourteen, and my own kid's in a home up near Syracuse somewhere."

He let her talk, calculating her changes, desperate to take her. But finally under him, thin bundle, feverish but slippery, eluding his rhythms, he caught a thin hum, monotonic, behind her tight lips as she squirmed. Afterwards she edged onto her side and buried her face in his shoulder. "Keep me covered," she whispered. "I'm hell on blankets, I squirm them off and then I wake up freezing." She woke him up crying, spasms which hinted at ritual, he kneaded her spiky shoulders and murmured *shah shah* into her hair, remembered nuzzling into the soft folds of his grandmother's neck. In the moments she stopped, exhausted, to catch her breath, he mopped her face with the same damp corner of the bedsheet, bullied her into blowing her nose, lit cigarettes for both of them and then finished hers as sobbing took her again, her knees arrowing into his thighs, her back muscles knotted under his fingers. When he guessed she was finally spent he wiped her face dry and kissed the tip of her nose. "I'm sorry, I know it's terrible." "Be quiet." Gruffly, his fingers working to ease the strained muscles hunching her shoulders. "I just can't tell, sometimes when I'm lucky I get through a whole week of nights but other times—" she shrugged. "This week it's every night so far."

His hands never stopped. Finally he took her again, persuaded she was eager. Quick pain which shifted as he whispered her name, he moved inside her gently, then less gently, his hands digging to reach her through her spare flesh. And took, instead, only her keen, high-pitched hum vibrating like some unmodulated frequency in his forehead. He clamped his teeth closed behind lips pressed into the tiny hollow of her shoulder blade and worked her, doggedly, insistent, finally with abandon, riding a rhythm threatening to split his eardrums. Provoked, her energy rose, sealed him, both sweaty, and rode down with him till his head split and he opened his mouth to gasp and moaned instead. His ears told him he was unrecognizable as his head slumped onto the pillow. He waited till his blood slowed, a long time, before he dared to look at her.

She was staring through the curtain at some dim light source, the moon or Anne-Marie's window where the light was always on. "Hey." And stroked her arm. She didn't turn. "It's scary." And later, after she snuggled down again: "Don't forget to cover me up or I'll freeze you in the morning, my toes go actually blue." And just before she fell asleep: "I'll be all right now, I really will, you don't have to worry." She woke him again just after dawn. She wasn't crying but he took her anyway.

Phone jarred him. Stumbled into the kitchen, stubbed his toe on Laurie's stool and knocked it over, then flinched for the grandmother downstairs, pounding at the pipes. "I promised I'd call, I didn't mean to wake you. Everything was perfect, your wife'll be in the Recovery Room for about forty minutes." He mumbled apologies at the crisp voice, unable to complete a sentence. "Well, I think if you hurried you might make it up here before they bring her back to her room. I've left word for you to be admitted, you could even see her in the Recovery Room if you got up here fast enough. I'm sorry I woke you, but I've still got my gown on." Mumbled his thanks. "Everything did go well, as well as we expected. Better. She won't have much difficulty healing. But you'll see for yourself." "Thanks," he managed finally, and groped the receiver back onto its cradle. Three miles uptown swaddled in bandages, flat on a rolling stretcher down a flatly lit hallway, tube beside her dripping liquid into her veins. Thick colorless liquid. Below her stomach, under layers of jellied padding, an angry red gash was trickling blood, held together by clamps which forced a ridgeline of raw flesh. He stumbled back to bed wanting only an hour's dumb sleep and encountered her thin warmth, solicitous. Surprisingly they found more than a respite, he smiled at her, tentatively, as they finished a cigarette. "You've got to go somewhere." And kissed his shoulder, quick child's peck. "You've got to go somewhere you don't want to go." And at his wrinkle of surprise: "It's never hard to guess things like that. Go look at your face in the mirror." And with her icy feet she pushed him out of bed. "I look like that every morning," he shouted from the kitchen, "just let me shower and then I'll buy you breakfast." Caught himself singing under the spray. Hospital odors would cover any scent on his flesh and besides, Laurie was in no condition to sniff after him. Exactly, he grinned, and so couldn't decide why, as he watched her chew soggy forkfuls of scrambled egg, he wouldn't ask her to stay on. For a few days, at least, she could use the footing. "Where will you go?" Shrugged, sipping lukewarm coffee, staring past him at the empty counter. "Uptown. Left my clothes with a friend." "And then?" "Oh, I dunno. Downtown, maybe. I got friends on the East Side, there's plenty of floors around. I'll think about it later." Implying he was a nuisance, put up or shut up. But staring at her vacant frown he decided she'd intended nothing, had already consigned him. He kissed her forehead for goodbye on the subway steps and watched her wander up the avenue, schoolgirl ankles. Only two stops uptown he was regretting letting her go, twisting her under him as the car lurched and bucked, why sleep alone? Sallow in coarse cotton, her hand limp in his, he watched Laurie's eyelids quiver. "She'll be coming round soon," the nurse whispered. "It all went very well. She came out of it once when they transferred her and she called for you, but it was only for a second and then she dropped right off again." You make sure everybody pays, don't you? Nodded his thanks, never antagonize nurses. When Laurie started to whimper he murmured her name; through her hazy sense of the pain awaiting her she tried to smile and her dry lips cracked as they parted, so he sponged first her lips and then her forehead with square gauze pads soaking in an aluminum tray whose kidney shape offended him. "It hurts! Oh god it hurts so much!" Hours she whimpered and sobbed, drifting toward consciousness where the pain was too searing to be borne. They let him stay till late into the evening, most of her normal color had returned but the anesthetic had ebbed, leaving her defenseless. She soaked his handkerchief. He remembered that the bedsheet corner might still be damp. "I'm such a coward, I know, but I just can't stand it!" Helpless, he finally shuffled out to beg. "Can't you give her something?" Watched the needlepoint plunge into her thigh, shivered as the plunger jammed some ten hours' sleep into her. When she went under, old lady's wheeze like his grandmother's, he kissed her glassy cheek and tiptoed away, not only thanked the nurses but reminded himself to tip them, too, in case Laurie's pain made her short-tempered. Walked all the way home to numb himself, his mind closed to everything except traffic sounds and the first six bars of "Bye Bye Blackbird," he kept whistling variations as he trudged downtown. By morning her smells

30

were faint on his sheets, only the kitten he rescued, cringing in an overcrowded cage, preserved her. He swore to one of the hags who ran the shop that he'd have it altered as soon as it reached its doubtful maturity, a promise he figured he'd enjoy breaking, and then fed it and soothed its wobblings through the ten days Laurie took to learn the limits of her wound. When he finally brought Laurie home, the kitten had mastered its box, could locate its food and hide successfully in all their cupboards and closets. Vulnerable tortoise-shell, uncertain markings, spontaneous legs and tail, bizarre navigation and a consistently cold nose which homed on sensitive flesh. It mewed plaintively as he set Laurie down; had it learned its name? "This is Tattoo." He cupped a hand under its thin belly and plopped it, trembling, into Laurie's lap. She cried as she cuddled it.

Tunneling back into bed after Laurie's phone call, he wondered why they hadn't considered it more of an evil omen when Tattoo died. Maybe Laurie never realized how much I meant her for exorcism. Laurie was so positive the old hag downstairs had poisoned her, but that's crazy, she'd have had to sneak up here to feed her and we always keep the door locked. Maybe Laurie thinks she lured Tattoo down by the fire escape? You don't have to imagine conspiracies, he chided Laurie, there's enough real ones going on in this building. He fell asleep worrying whether Sal was working day shift again.

SAL *Evans was on the desk when Jones and Dolan brought him in. "Hello, Dutch," I says. I decided to book him myself as soon as I seen his face. Every cop knows the look.*

Some guys brazen it out, put up a tough front knowing that their

31

fancy lawyer, the one who they pay a fat monthly retainer, is due any minute to bail them out and put together a story that'll stand up in court. We're too busy to be perfect, if you got enough money you can probably beat us. But nobody showed up to bail him out, you might buy him a drink at Tony's or a cup of coffee at the club, but that don't make him part of the neighborhood when it comes to bail. Which woulda been steep, anyway, I couldn't list him for less than manslaughter and even then I was taking a chance. Angie thinks I always figure the percentages before I stick my neck out, but how often does one of your own wind up on the wrong side of the cage? The Lieutenant wouldn't pass it, worried we'd get accused of playing soft with our own. "We'll have a goddam delegation sitting in on our steps as soon as we announce the charges." "Fuck 'em," I growled but it wouldn't wash. "List him for second degree, till we see what turns up," the Lieutenant said, he's a political appointment with ambitions, plays everything tight and keeps his fingers crossed. So I listed him for second degree, but nothing turned up, nothing connected the two of them except the fact that she lived upstairs, he didn't even know her name! Lissen, if I found something I sure as hell mighta salted it away, difference of six to ten years, depending on probation, which he won't get, he coulda been out of the state before we found her but he never tried to get away. Those kids of hers woulda sat there all day, too dumb to cry. Of all the goddam people to pick! You're gonna knock one of them off, at least pick somebody useful. We got plenty down here could stand getting rid of, each cop has his own list. But a woman with five kids minds her own business, what the hell's the point, even if she was a nigger? "Now look, Dutch," I told him, I hadda steady his elbow to guide him into the back room, "the main thing you gotta understand is that you got a long pull ahead of you, lotta orders to take, lotta places to go, lotta people taking your picture and your fingerprints and your blood, it makes for confusion. You're gonna be in a long time and rule number one is that nobody's in a hurry, just relax every chance you get." Kept staring at his hands. I asked if he was hungry but he didn't answer. I spoon-fed him some soup anyway, after he wiped his chin he kept opening his mouth like a fish. He already had that smell they get. "You wanna see a priest, Dutch? We can get Father Angelo down here inside a half hour. Or anybody else you want." Hadda shut the cage on him, I almost apologized but he never noticed, slumped on the bench, nodding his head. An hour later he was asleep in the same position, his chin wedged into his chest. So when I finally got some free time to see the Counselor, I guess I poured it on a little. "Look, with all due respect for the fact that it ain't my business and I'm taking a chance just to mention it to you, I wouldn't leave a guy like that for Legal Aid to represent." "We'll take up a collection," the Counselor rumbled. "I'm sure he was known and loved throughout the neighborhood." "For Chrissake," I mumbled, I'd never had much respect for the Counselor's shrewdness, "I'm not talking about charity. I'm trying to imagine what a guy like that knows. He's already half outa his head, suppose he gets resentful and his tongue works loose, who shuts him up? I can't guarantee it, totally depends on who's on duty Suppose he remembers a couple details about some job he was used on, uptown or downtown, if the wrong sergeant's on the desk the newspapers got another story. Now I'll admit I don't keep my ear so close to the ground any more, but even I know that Parisi used him on some uptown runs, and Freddie and the Duke picked him up for lots of small jobs. If I know that much, he must be a gold mine. And you're letting him sit there, maybe he's stewing because nobody cares whether he's still alive, and he's got enough information floating around in his head to convict half the neighborhood. Suppose he makes a deal? We don't really want him, we'll probably let him plead to manslaughter to

33

save us a trial, if he starts feeding us information we might drop all his charges. Why take the chance? Send one of your new college boys to bail him out, prepare a decent case. The DA don't have a scrap of motive, he even used her goddam frying pan."

Counselor's a cornball, rotates his White Owl like it was Havana, stares at the ash like he was judging pearls till it falls off the tip from its own weight. "Sal, you're right, it makes sense. I'll look into it. And I want you to know I appreciate a man on the force who still cares about the old neighborhood. And keeps his eyes open."

"Think nothing of it, Counselor," I said, "but I gotta be going, I'm overdue on the desk and I never signed out." And got the hell outa his office before he tried to hand me a couple of bills he looked ready to peel off. Just a token of my esteem, he'd probably say. If I depended on guys like the Counselor I'd be pounding pavements out in Queens. When they brought Dutch into the precinct, I knew it was up to me to help him out, he couldn't do nothing for himself. A born loser. Detective came in with her picture somebody dug up outa some city file, he didn't even recognize her. Dolan questioned her kids, only thing he got outa them was they thought Dutch was the exterminator! The goddam exterminator comes twice a year to buildings like that, three times if they're really lucky. But you know how it is, the exterminator's white, and Dutch's white, we all look alike to them.

Disturbance at the nurses' desk spilled him up out of the chop
of the Chesapeake Bay. Squat Puerto Rican woman, plaits
looped and pinned into coils at the nape of her neck, screamed
as she battled a trio of nurses wedging her away from the
elevators. Two orderlies raced across the cracked concrete
floor, pinned her arms, then frog-marched her down a hallway.
Matto yawned into the back of his hand, his canvas deck
chair creaking, its cloth bleached white from sun and salt
spray, stitching already powder in half the tucks. Everything's
rotting, Balzano says at least three times a day. Need a good
woman on board for a month of mending. Or a weary sailor
with a nimble thimble.

*The girl straddled Balzano, stomach and hips pumping against
the bright blue of his saddle-stitched trousers. His thick fingers
squeezed her buttocks, each cheek firmly gripped and then sponged,
creased, kneaded, drawn taut and released. Wind stirred her short
blond hair. The cone of her right breast squashed against Balzano's
checked sportshirt as her narrowed eyes stared at Matto.*

Who had come up from the cabin to find them, balanced on
the stern swivel chair, the girl's head draped over Balzano's
left shoulder, her eyes slitted and her tongue's tip sliding across
her protruding front teeth as she breathed in slow, sucking
gasps. He watched until her eyes widened. In a flat, casual
tone: "Hey, who's that?"

Balzano twisted, spilling her sideways but pinning her left leg
and thigh and steadying her ass with his big hands so he stayed
inside her. Matto, swallowing, saw he was still chewing his
cigar.

35

"Nothing. Don't worry about him." Spat out his chewed-off ends. "He don't see nothing. Or say nothing." And with no exasperation: "Whatsa matter, didn't I tell you to stay down below?"

"Yeah."

"So stay down below."

A satisfied grunt and Matto, as he turned, saw hairy hands twisting the girl back over him, breasts swaying as she reared, suspended, then wriggled and sank down. Matto, straining to see, caught her eyes slit and unfocus, tongue beginning to squirm across her outcrop of teeth, then he was too far down the hatchway, ridge of deck floor cut off his view. He shuffled across the damp cabin floor to the engine hatch, watched the generator throwing sparks without worrying any more whether the main lines would short before they reached the coast, and jerked off, letting his jit spatter the water-soaked walls and join the brine in the washways. As he got close, pressure in his temples creased his forehead, he narrowed his eyes and worked his tongue over the cutting edges of his teeth, hearing her flat voice call him *sugar* like the girls in Luzon. Balzano let him alone till evening.

Balzano threw private parties maybe four times a season. After the '48 summer he always took Matto, the girls cooked and Balzano mixed his own drinks, with no fish to prepare for market it was always an easy weekend. Two girls, usually; Balzano could afford to pamper himself, and for the girls it was almost a vacation, two nights on the open sea, $50 a weekend plus eats and drinks and a good sunburn. They teetered on board in white slacks and heavy gray sweatshirts,

slept on deck unless the Carolina squalls caught them, and
changed into bikinis after Saturday morning breakfast. Matto
stayed below deck, washed the dishes, nursed the engine, and
made the same slow run through the channel and out to weigh
anchor some thirty miles northeast of the Cape, the fishing
fleets headed south and then southeast off Hatteras. The girls
turned sluggish, windburned and parched by Saturday sunset,
so Matto served as a stolid fourth for rummy; never mix
women and poker, Balzano had warned him on Luzon.
Drugged by the sun and the salt which caked their lips and
the fading lines of their eye makeup, their skins burning under
heavy sweatshirts and coarse blankets, the girls yawned over
their highballs, blinked in the flickering light of the Coleman
lantern, smiled hazily at Matto, called him *sweetie* and *lamb*,
patted his forearm and shoulder and dropped swiftly into sleep.
Balzano snored, his massive head propped against the liquor
cabinet. Once, although Matto never remembered, Balzano
sent him a girl who slipped down the narrow hatchway ladder
to Matto's post at the wheel.

"Gus says I should talk to you."

Matto grunted, hands clenched on the spokes though her
anchor was forty feet down, dragging rock. Beneath her top
the girl was built small, Matto watched them quiver as she
smoothed the wet lengths of her hair into a matted pony tail,
then ran a sure forefinger across the hairs of his right forearm.

"So?" she said.

"Gus is a good guy. I'm working for him." Matto's left hand
slid off the wheel, thinking he heard Gus's bulk squeaking the
springs of his swivel chair. Elastic webbing molding her suit

37

taut across her hips was beginning to dry but her flanks were still wet. Matto traced the line of her thigh to the curls of hair escaping from the damp V her suit pressed into her crotch. Sea spray, still moist on her knees and calves, blotted his fresh white ducks as she leaned closer to him.

"Sure Uncle Gus is a good guy. That's why he sent me down here. He don't feel good about you being left out of the party. Tell him he can afford to relax a little, Uncle Gus says. Tell him he's off duty from now on, his working day's over." Her fingers exploring his right arm slipped under his jersey, traced the mottled lumps of his scar. "Were you in the war too? With Uncle Gus in the Pacific?" Matto nodded. "Well, look, you gotta promise me one thing, just don't talk about it, okay? I am so fed up with war stories, I swear to God if I hear another one I'll jump overboard and swim back to shore."

Matto could've kept his mouth shut. The girl didn't require conversation, and Uncle Gus had slipped her an extra $20 hinting that Matto might still be virgin. But instead he shook his head. "I don't talk about the war. Ever. I don't talk about nothing. They just want me to stand around and do things for them."

The girl stopped laughing when she saw his face and for more than ten minutes she watched his Adam's apple bob as he swallowed phlegm. Her fault, she decided. Some guys had memories they still couldn't deal with. Balzano decided she actually fell for him, but more likely it was pity, such a slow tongue, bashful face as he stared at the sea. "C'mon," she whispered finally and slipped her arm around his waist. "I'm getting cold, and afterwards for dinner I'll make you some of my special fish soup, you'll feel a whole lot better." But afterwards they fell asleep beneath heavy wool blankets. The girl forgot her soup because Matto handled her too roughly, and Matto snored through sunset.

Sprawled flat on the bow, toes of his sneakers wedged under a coil of flaking rope, Matto lets the sun bake him, dozes. Beneath his stomach he can feel the whunk as the bow takes the chop.

"Matto." The vaulted ceiling echoes it. "Matto!" Peremptory.

Matto almost wakes, rush of dirty light which crumbles sea and horizon, spirals his stomach upward. But twisting his shoulder into the slatted wooden bench he grunts, finds the boat again, skims at water level, spray blinding him, pressure constricting his chest as he squints, licking his salty lips. The wind roars in his ears, his hair is plastered to his forehead, the clot in his chest stirs, unknots, and dissolves through his stomach, down into his bowels coarses a hot flow that warms his thighs and calves before streaming into the coil of rope. A gull eases onto a whitecap, wings braked like flaps, claws extended to rinse beneath the chop. Somersaults, and its head and neck plunge, reappear, no fish wriggling in its beak. The gull wheels upward, folding its leg to its slicked white breast, shrill hoarse cries.

"Matto." Crisp, angry. "Matto!"

Matto wakes. His temples throb. Dirty light-globes sway on quivering chains from the vaulted ceiling, and stretched into rows of benches, too many bent yellow necks.

39

"Matto! Last call!"

"Yes. Here. Here." His hands lock, brace against bench back. His good leg slides, stiffens, and straightens to jack up the other. As his right knee gingerly unlocks he finds the floor with his right toe and half shuffles, half drags, into the aisle. Waiting rows blur as he edges past, wobbly on sloping floor to the white-coated black orderly at the barrier.

"You Matto?"

"Yeah."

"You deaf? Called your name seven times!"

"I fell asleep. I got up at six—to come here."

"Yeah? Well I got up at five, buddy, same as every morning, and I'll be here long after you're gone, so don't sweat it. This is people's medicine, buddy, be thankful it's here at all!" Bloodshot behind his owlish horn rims, his eyes already registered Matto's limp and the dark stain spreading from Matto's crotch across his right pants leg.

Matto traced the slants and curls of writing he thought spelled his name on the manila folder. "They fix up my knee today?"

Through the barrier gate into the chair, witness chair, orderly filling out the usual forms. "Same address?" Matto didn't bother to nod. "Roll up your right pants leg. How come you wet yourself?"

Matto's cuff catches on a roll of flesh, a flicker of pain jabs into his bulbous knee. He forces the fraying trouser edges over the hump of swollen knee and up his thigh, then stares at the

40

stain matting his right leg, trousers clammy, soggy underwear sticking to his balls. "I was asleep." And tries to shrug.

"You just couldn't hold it. Maybe you had a nice dream." Orderly's eyes catch the flush creeping up Matto's neck. "Forget it. They'll clean you up, upstairs. Let's see that knee." Matto looked, too. White crown of flesh, impacted mass of fluid shifting beneath taut skin. Angry flush. Matto braced the cap with his thumbs and flexed the lower leg. The cap's slide was barely visible, a crease beneath thick fluids. The orderly nodded as Matto eased his cuff down, pen scratching across the form clamped into his folder. "Looks bad." A grudged respect. "How'd you do it?"

Hesitated, licked his lips. "Bus door—close on me. I run for the bus, see it halfway down the block. Driver don't see me. One foot on the step, door close—whoosh!" Collapsing motion with both hands, concertina pushed inwards. "I fall backwards. Catch this one," tapping the thigh of his bad leg, "underneath me."

Just make up a story, tell them anything, they're too busy to give a damn, the doctor said. Freddie and Morello took him to somebody who wouldn't ask questions, not that they had any real worries. Surplus ammo, cartridge cases, packed in regulation U.S. Army boxes. Besides he couldn't read. "Hey Dutch, you wanna make ten bucks, we need a hand shifting some stuff tomorrow." Rented truck in a Queens driveway, those black bastards ever come up here we'll blow their heads off. Case of grenades balanced on his shoulder, packed in straw like tropical fruit, pins securely sealed, he twists his ankle on a loose slab of paving that Freddie is always promising to fix

41

because his wife hates the lurch when she's backing her
Pontiac out of the garage, she's always certain she's got another
flat. Matto lost his balance but fell shielding the case, which
slid off his right shoulder and crushed the knee already bent
beneath him. "He should've dropped the case," Freddie said
afterwards, "he didn't have a clue what was inside, what'd
he think he was saving? We never told him he was carrying
perfume. Or eggs. Worst thing coulda happened, the case
would split and he'd see a coupla grenades. Big deal." They
figured he was okay till they watched him limp to the truck,
he couldn't sit with his knee bent, they moved over to give
him leg room. Doctor shook his head, gave him Cortisone
tablets. "For the swelling. These should bring it down a little.
But I think you shattered part of the kneecap. Stay off it.
When the swelling goes down, go to the clinic and
get it X-rayed. They'll do it for nothing. I'd have to
charge you."

By rights they should've put him into a hospital, Freddie knew
what clinics are like. A week in semi-private, three meals a
day, clean sheets, not to mention the nurses, would've given
Matto his first real vacation, not counting the Army. But he
was always banging himself up, Freddie figured, never seen
him when he wasn't limping. If he'da just let the case drop
instead of trying to play hero, he'd be okay. Or at least, no
worse than usual. Which, Freddie figured, wasn't worth that
much, certainly not two weeks in a hospital. So Freddie forced
an extra $10 on Matto before they dropped him off, Morello
scowled as he watched Matto drag his right leg across the
empty street. "You don't think there's a chance he'll open his
mouth?" Freddie laughed, stuffing his billfold back into his

42

wallet pocket. "Who's he gonna talk to? Nobody knows he's alive."

The orderly stares. Matto decides he's said enough but still stares at his folder. "What does it say there, for my birthday?"

"August 28, 1914."

"1914." Matto mumbles the year again, pretending to subtract. "So if I was born in 1914—" "That makes you fifty-one. Next August you'll be fifty-two." The orderly waited, without fidgeting, Matto's file open beneath his knuckles, watching Matto trying to count to fifty-one on his fingers. Thinking a pile of toothpicks might be more useful, he actually reached into his desk drawer to see how full his toothpick box was.

"Leroy." His hand hesitated, caressed the cold drawer knob. His name in her mouth always demanded more than apology. *You have to watch them all the time, you can't trust them alone for one minute!* More controlled than the face from whose cheeks powder never quite concealed the flush, her voice pursued its advantage. "After six months in this department, you're still not aware that the information recorded in in-take files is never divulged to clients?"

Reluctantly he granted her a marginal withdrawal, fractional nod of his set jaw and chin. "I'm aware."

"Well?" Adamant. Pulse in the ridge of skin covering her high cheekbones registered her tension. *Wasn't she destined for more than this interminable squabbling with the colored help?* She forced herself to hold his look. *He's got such hate for me, he'd like to kill me. Or worse. Whenever you catch them, they defend*

43

themselves with insolence. "It doesn't matter," he said finally, flat tone, no hint of mollification. "He can't read."

"Then why is his file displayed so conveniently in front of him?"

april 7, 1965

Alonzo comes up for sentencing next week. When I wangled that pass which got me into the Tombs, the only thing he wanted to know was: "Did they find out?" I didn't have to lie, then. As far as I knew they hadn't.

re Alonzo Cobb—Probation Dept forwarded a copy of their report and recommendations. Looks bad. Too many convictions, he was still on probation from the last one.

I spotted him the first time I visited their apartment, asked him to walk me to the corner just as I was leaving, casually, but in front of the mother so he couldn't refuse. "You're on the needle, aren't you?" He was sixteen then, he glowered at me. "It's that plain? You don't look like you been around much." I wanted him to talk so I swallowed my morsel of pride and nodded. "You gonna tell my folks?"

He was waiting at home my next two visits, stoop-shouldered crouch by the kitchen radiator, some instinctual radar warned him when I'd come. By not betraying him I got sucked in. His next arrest I lived on the phone; to the family, the precinct, Legal Aid, I abandoned the rest of my caseload. "It'll kill my old man, it'll just finish him off for good."

From Probation Dept's report on Alonzo Cobb—Family seems a cut above average for that neighborhood, but father's disability has limited family's income, means, mobility, and contacts. Father seems to have been a preacher of some considerable reputation in neighborhood, is still an impressive figure in spite of his paralysis, which is severe. Mother says he is occasionally transported to his old church to give a guest sermon. Seems the nature of those type of churches

45

not to make any arrangements for their pastors. Mother said they took up a collection which only paid his hospital bill.

The first time I met the father I almost bowed, he seemed regal in his wheelchair, African blanket shrouding his crippled legs. "I'm sorry to trouble you, sir," I said, wishing I could disappear. "You've got a job to do, young man," he rumbled, "get on with it. Pride's a luxury for a man in my position. I'm thankful to the good Lord my head's still clear and my voice's still strong." His youngest son was his most bitter affliction; they dropped their voices as if softness excluded him, impassive, rocking on the radiator, while they begged me to concoct an administrative solution—a change of schools, a job-training program, anything that would set him back on the right path. "I suppose in your line of work you hear too many parents saying this, but I just can't believe I've brought my son up to be a common thief." Alonzo rode the radiator, bobbing his head. "He's not a common thief, he's just a kid with two busts for stealing. Every kid steals, it's part of growing up in this country. I stole plenty when I was a kid." And tried to grin. "How much harder you think it would be," I asked Alonzo once, "if they knew you were a junkie and had to think about you as a junkie instead of a thief, like your father says? You really think it'd be that much harder for them?"

Alonzo didn't react, hands shoved deep into his slash pockets, waited a half block before answering. I knew he'd heard. "I went to one of my daddy's sermons about three years ago. The last sermon I ever heard. Naturally he was talking about the needle. Know what he called us? Vermin. Said we was

46

worse than the rats whose bites killed little thumb-sucking
babies. Said we was the worst of the plagues which the Lord
Almighty had sent down to cleanse the black community, worse
than locusts, worse than boils, worse even than the destruction
of all the first-born because we were already zombies, walking
dead, and our touch turned everything to rot. Just how do
you think he's gonna take the good news that one of them
vermin been living in his house the past sixteen years?"

From Probation Dept's report on Alonzo Cobb—Accused
is sullen, noncommunicative, often hostile in direct exami-
nation and conversation. Volunteers nothing, often seeks
to evade even sympathetic questioning. Present attitude and
past record seem to indicate a chronic recidivist, a pattern
which school records, attempts at vocational guidance, and
previous probationary experience seem to bear out. Accused
has never evidenced a coherent and lasting interest in
anything, has never held a job, has no career goals, no long-
standing friends or older acquaintances he respects in the
community.

I finally spotted the lawyer I'd spent those two days on the
phone with, kid just out of Brooklyn Law, younger than his
voice, an accountant's son with a thin-lapeled continental-style
suit which hung, on him, as if it were waiting for his
confidence to expand in order to inhabit it. "You know how
soon they'll call Alonzo Cobb's case?" Blinked, nervously
shuffling a scrambled sheaf of arrest sheets. "So you're the
one's been breaking my ear for two days! Boy, I couldn't get
any other work done, my supervisor said to tell you Legal Aid
is not DW's law service. When you want individual attention
you gotta hire somebody." Said with no passion, already

47

*blinking at the overhead lights, the rows of uniformed and
plainclothes cops, the trio of Assistant DA's. I was tempted
to grab his thin lapels and shove my chin into his face. "You
can tell your supervisor to shove it up his ass," I growled.
"And I'll put that in writing, on whatever forms he wants.
Now look, concentrate for a minute. They got Alonzo on
Assault on a Police Officer, Possession and Use of heroin,
Breaking and Entering, Possession of Stolen Property. The
only charge they can actually prove is the last one, the other
three are bullshit, you've seen the sheet. He gave the arresting
officer some lip when he came through the door, no warrant
was ever issued, the whole bust was illegal. All they found
was a rusty needle and an empty cartridge, they never even got
it lab-tested, for all they knew he was diabetic and the kit
was for insulin." He rolled his eyes. "Oh, come on," he said.
"We know the kid's an addict." I grabbed his shoulder and
shook him, hard, wanting to ram my fist through his teeth,
cause him expensive bridgework take him years to pay off,
ashamed to open his mouth even to grin at superiors. "You
come on, you chicken-shit son of a bitch. This is an adversary
proceeding and you are the fucking defense lawyer, not the
goddam prosecution. You sound like the DA, buddy, he
assumes guilt, you assume innocence. You read his record,
legally he is not an addict, if there was a lawyer defending
Alonzo instead of a clay pigeon for the DA's office, they'd
have to prove that stuff in the cartridge was smack! And they
can't do it. They can't prove use, either; all they got is a small
collection of old hash marks on his right arm. And for the
Assault charge they'll have to stick the cop on the stand,
DA's office doesn't like convictions on one cop's testimony.
All you have to do is open your mouth and pretend you're*

*about to make a fight and they'll drop those charges before you
finish your first sentence. It won't cost you anything to act
like a lawyer for a change, instead of a eunuch!" Just kept
blinking at me, smoothed his lapel after I let go his jacket.
At least he understood I was desperate. I never saw him in
conference with the Assistant DA, but when he waggled me
over he seemed almost pleased. "Okay, we got a deal. But it's
not on the property rap, DA wouldn't settle for that. Wants
another Breaking and Entering to be sure the kid's sent away.
Also some question of insurance. Most he'll do is drop the
other three for Breaking and Entering."*

From Probation Dept's report on Alonzo Cobb—Parents
professed ignorance as to Accused's status as addict. Mother
in particular swore her son "never touched the needle."
Father kept issuing flat denials, implied either worker or
record was mistaken. Both parents admitted knowledge of
their son's record of theft, etc., but both denied any
knowledge of what the thefts might have been for. Both
denied Accused spent any time in Rhb Ward, though
Accused's record shows three two-week periods spent
specifically in Rehabilitation. Worker tried to convince both
parents that it was to their advantage, as well as their son's,
to cooperate, since the final Probation Report, which would
affect the sentencing, would reflect their attitudes. Neither
parent changed their story They both insisted, throughout
the interview, that their son could not possibly be an addict.

*"What do you want to do?" I asked Alonzo once. We were
both sitting on our asses, our backs propped up against a
concrete playground wall. Alonzo was waiting out a four-
on-four game, the losers would drop a man, and me—I was*

49

*taking my ease. A hot Thursday in July, asphalt spongy
underfoot, only in uptown is basketball played in 90° weather.
I'd sprung Alonzo from home and I wasn't in any hurry
to get to my next visit. "Whatta you mean?" he said finally.
"What I said. You ever think about getting clear of all this
and doing something—something that's maybe very different
but something you really want to do?" He snickered. I didn't
blame him. "You mean, like rob a bank, get enough to live
the rest of my life on?" I grinned. "Yeah, something like that."
We both watched a rebound clear and the ball passed out and
then in to the big center, who faked left, faked right, started
a dribble off the key to his right, faked a drive, stopped, faked
a jumper, then took it. The ball bounced high off the front
rim, fell away. We'd both been certain he'd miss it. "You
know what I'd really like to do?" He was mumbling, I had
to strain to hear him. "I'd like to get the hell outa here, get to
one of the islands, St. Kitts or St. Thomas, get me something
good going there and never have to think about this place
again." I waited through three quick baskets. "By this place
you mean this country?" Snorted. "I ain't even seen this
country. I ain't even seen this city, 'cept for a little bit of the
Bronx and uptown and the East River Drive when they took
me to Rehab. I don't expect to see much more, either, 'less
they send me upstate to the big pen. Most of my traveling the
next dozen years or so be on the government."*

*His trial was too quick for farce. The bailiff called his case
in a jumble of words which somehow both the cop next to
Alonzo and the Legal Aid lawyer deciphered, the cop shoved
Alonzo onto his feet and pointed him in the direction of the
bench and the lawyer, semaphoring his arrest sheets. Before*

Alonzo had reached the stand the lawyer was already explaining his guilty plea; in the pause after the Judge asked the DA "whether the People found that plea acceptable" I held my breath, expecting a double-cross. "Stand up straight there, you!" the Judge barked at Alonzo. "And get your hands out of your pockets, nobody slouches in my courtroom!" Once the Assistant DA accepted the plea it was all over, the Judge set May 2 for sentencing. I watched Alonzo stumble back through the pen to disappear behind the wood-paneled doors which led to the temporary cages and finally to the Tombs. He didn't turn around. The most I could do now was send his mother a note listing visiting hours, what he would say if she ever showed up was outside my responsibility. I sent the whole file in for transfer to another section without checking with Carson.

In the A & P to do Laurie's shopping, he realized he'd made no list, bumped into Angie's cart in the cereal aisle, dazed at his possibilities. Have you been watching me bumbling through this maze? "Good morning." And grinned. "You know you look just as good in the daylight. In fact better. More tempting."

She poked a stubby finger at him. "You watch your mouth or I'll report you to the manager." *He looks\ youngest in the mornings, lean, unbutton his shirt to make him shiver under my fingers. I went up on the roof with a robe loose over my nightgown and he was over by the chimneys, gloomy, waiting for sunrise but he could hardly keep his eyes open. When he cupped his hands to light my cigarette I smelled his skin and knew I wanted to screw him.*

LAURIE   *In the beginning when he couldn't sleep I blamed myself. I never imagined he went looking for it like some alleycat, sniffing. He walked the streets trying to tell himself how important it was to be alive, collecting his little nighttime vignettes for buttress. When he jarred me awake, deliberately as often as not, climbing into bed sometimes long after dawn, I could always feel his contempt. While the real world uncoiled before him, all I chose was my sleep.*

"I don't like leaving Nikky alone, she wakes up so scared sometimes she'd scream herself into hysterics if I wasn't there. But it's so goddam hot in my place! Even with those two window fans Sal rigged up. At least you're in the front of the building, you get the breeze off the river."

"When it comes." Watching the flimsy collar of her nightgown ride up to brush her neck as she turned from the parapet to grind out her cigarette. "Even then it's just as hot." Quick

53

hellos on the stoop, imprint of firm thigh as she brushed past him on the stairs, nothing he remembered about the building's judgments of her added up to prohibition. "Sometimes when it's hot like this I walk all night, down to the Battery, past the ferry slips to the docks, up to the Fish Market, then through the projects and Chinatown. Sometimes I play a game, I count everybody I meet and once I pass twenty-five I can go home. Except I never count cops. Doesn't seem fair." Hesitant to risk touch, but not apprehensive, certain he sniffed her heat. "How'd you meet Sal?"

ANGIE   *I almost laughed. Everybody knew Sal stayed with me, but he had to whisper, confidential, like he'd already told me the story of his life. So I said, "He picked me up for soliciting and after I gave him a free sample he decided it'd be cheaper in the long run not to turn me in." He yawned and brushed his hair out of his eyes. "What'd you expect, the story of my life at four in the morning?" "Why not?" he said. "You know a better time?" His shirt was open enough to see there wasn't any hair on his chest, no bush like Sal's. But lean, the skin stretched tight so you could see the outlines of bone. I shrugged my shoulders and moved closer, he had enough reasons to be shy and I wasn't in any hurry, Nikky never wakes up till eight. "It's sure as hell a long story," I said, just to warn him—*

—you only moved in here two, three years ago, you don't know the neighborhood. I grew up here and moved away and came back with a kid and no marriage certificate, they're still scared of me so they only call Nikky a bastard behind my back. And her back. It was only after the attacks started I realized how much they freeze me out. Only by accident I found out, I met the mother of the third girl he got to. I never go to the laundromat that late but Nikky needed

54

a uniform I was too lazy to wash by hand so I figured what the hell, get a whole load done. It was pretty clear she needed to talk, she couldn't stop crying. After I loaded up three machines and put my bleach in I sat down beside her, she wasn't more than twenty-five. She always let her kid downstairs to play on the sidewalk in front of the building, hanging halfway out her window like I watch Nikky. What happened to her was a friend called up so she spent twenty minutes gabbing. As soon as she put the phone down she had a pre-monition, craned her head out the window and couldn't find her so she raced downstairs and there was her little girl whimpering on the first-floor landing, her panties off and her dress stained. Six and a half, a year older than Nikky was then, the cops said he was the kind never even chased them once they ran away. Just coaxed them into a corner, got their panties off and came between their legs; he got into a couple of the older ones enough to make them bleed. I went crazy. Nikky was five minutes late coming home from school I was already on the phone to the precinct, once she forgot to walk home with Toni and Sandra and I grabbed her wrists so hard to shake her my fingers left deep red gouges in her skin. The old people tried to shush me, clucking like chickens, why couldn't I keep my mouth shut? "Don't worry, Gina, the police'll get him." Three quiet weeks and then three more attacks in the same block, one in Blumenthal's building with those big fluorescent lights. Everywhere I went people tried to shut me up. "What can we do?" they wanted to know. He hadda be from the neighborhood. Little girls all over the city, why else come back to the same three blocks? That was the first time I called the precinct, which sent a stupid detective to butter me up, fat pig of an Irishman thought he was hot shit with women, wouldn't keep his hands off me till I slapped him. Then he pretended to take down everything I said, gave me his personal phone number, just what I wanted. I stewed for two days, called the precinct back and told them they didn't come up with the guy in a week I'd talk to the papers about the kind of detectives they sent out to molest defenseless mothers. That's when they sent Sal. He didn't take any notes and he let me talk and he kept his hands on the table, but I wasn't very impressed. First thing he tells me after I've shot my mouth off is they've known for weeks it's some guy from the neighborhood but they can't find him. I laughed in his face. "Bullshit, Sergeant, I been around too long to believe you guys couldn't get him if you wanted him bad enough. Who you protecting?" He took his time, I remember noticing right away how carefully he follows your talk, you can watch him listening. But I didn't believe him. "Lissen," he said finally, "we want that guy inside, one of these days he's gonna pick on the wrong little girl and I'm out on Flushing Bay. We can't find him. Everybody's clammed up on us." He was right. "Gina," they told me, "how can we say anything, he's one of ours!" The same rules they'd always understood. And what about the little girls he gets in the hallways, I screamed, they're not ours? They're orphans? "It's a sickness, Gina, a sickness. It's not his fault." Like cancer. They couldn't say the name. Whisper a prayer on Sunday and maybe it'll go away, maybe everything bad will go away, hold your breath and cross yourself and maybe tomorrow everything will be better, what can we do? If he's sick the cops'll get him committed, I shouted, some kind of mental hospital's what he needs. You're protecting a monster, I yelled at them. Nobody's safe, how do you know he won't try to shove it into your granddaughter? "He won't touch her, he promised!" Covered her mouth with her hand but not quick enough. If he ever gets to my daughter, I told her, you better watch your kid like a hawk because I'll get to her, I'll fix her face so good you'll have to make her a nun because no man'll look at her without shivering. After the last attack I marched down to Tony's on a Friday afternoon, Sal told me that's when the Counselor's boys

56

give out the payroll. Lissen, I told them, if all the mothers in this neighborhood were crazy enough to let it get this far, I ain't crazy enough to let it go farther. You're all sick, but my kid ain't gonna be ruined on account of you. If I don't find out in two days who he is, me and however many mothers I can find who care more about their kids than about this fucking neighborhood are gonna parade up and down Grand Street with signs saying STOP PROTECTING SEX PERVERTS! LET OUR DAUGHTERS GROW UP NORMAL! Even if I'm the only one picketing, the papers will still show up, and I'll give them the names of everybody in this goddam neighborhood who won't open their mouths—including the Counselor. I'll bust this neighborhood wide open! You take your choice! Tony told me months later that I was screaming. All I remember is the hum from a bad neon connection over Tony's mirror when I finished, and a hand catching my elbow to steady me, gently, when I tripped over somebody's big feet on my way out. Three hours later I found a note in my mailbox. Just his name. Typewritten. When I called Sal I told him it might be a trap, or else a way to shut me up for a while. But they put a tail on him anyway, and four days later they caught him trying to get a little girl into Bernardi's alley behind the bakery. A couple mothers thanked me, that's all. The rest of the neighborhood hated my guts. I even got those chickenshit phone calls that wake you up in the middle of the night, they let you hear their breathing but they're too scared to say anything. Sal told me a long time later he put a twenty-four-hour watch on me, the word around the neighborhood was I hadda be taught a lesson. He even told the Counselor to lay off me, the Counselor kidded him for falling in love at his age and Sal said he just stuck his lower lip out, trying to play tough, while all the time he could feel the back of his neck burning under his heavy collar. He'd been around plenty after his wife ran off, but he never tried to hurry

57

me; the few mornings he didn't come by I missed bumping into his big coat swinging in the hallway, he wrapped his fingers clear around his coffee cup. So one morning after I got Nikky off to school I leaned over his shoulder to pour his second cup of coffee like I always did, but when I set the pot down I put my hand on his neck. He wasn't slow. They caught the guy four years ago this June—

Later the kid would acquire, untransformed, Sal's habit of nodding comprehension. Now as Angelina rambled he stared carefully at her eyes, avoiding her body, frowned at the roof's crumpling tar covering when he guessed his attention imposing on her narrative. As her eyes fixed and then unfocused he imagined them rolling up toward her drooping lids as she squirmed beneath him. Steamy bedroom, too many drapes and curtains, they never open their windows. Sal's lair? Maybe the kid pads in to punch two lumps under the blankets, giggle good morning. He grinned, unexpected benefit from Laurie's reserve after months of chafing at her ineptness in befriending the building's gossipy women. "It's late. Nikky'll be up soon." She sounded tired, was it dismissal or a search for a cigarette that sent her right hand probing her robe pocket? "Want one of mine? They're French, they're very strong. They're not really French, but they taste like the French ones. Try one." As she hesitated, he wedged the pack out of his shirt pocket, brushed her arm in offer, surprised at the fatigue in his tone. She let herself momentarily encircle his fingers, deciding he wasn't so scrawny after all. "Strong? Jesus, they're worse than cigars!" Fit of coughing exaggerated long after the tickle in her throat had subsided, she flicked the cigarette over the parapet, shower of sparks they both traced, cradled his forearm to steady herself. "Thanks." Her hair grazed his cheek, her

58

weight into the arc his arms completed when they took her shoulders. Held her loosely, fingers splayed across the nape of her neck, but staring down into her face he saw nothing to make him hesitate. Perhaps he felt slightly cheated. "We should go downstairs," she whispered into his neck. They disengaged, walked to the stairwell, she didn't trouble to take his hand. "I got neighbors so nosy they even stop watching television when I have visitors. No use giving them more ammunition." Downstairs he followed her through a hallway cluttered with coats and Nikky's toys and tricycle to her bedroom, where she grinned up at him, accomplices. "I never thought, all the times I seen you on the stoop or down at Rocco's, that we'd wind up in here. Did you? Ever?" He admitted both that he hadn't and that their pairing was, in some unspecifiable way, funny; chuckling, he stripped off his clothes, realizing he'd had no time to worry himself about whether he'd fail her and now he was already aroused, her plump but surprisingly thin-waisted body curved toward him as he knelt on her rumpled sheets. Afterwards, staring, shallow breaths barely stirring the stray hairs he thought should tickle her nose, he wondered why she never mentioned Laurie. Angelina—odd old-fashioned name, he whispered it and the bedroom swallowed it, he winked at his shadow slatted onto her ribbed bedspread and fell asleep.

"Lissen, Laurie's away for the whole weekend, okay if I come down tonight?" Watching her hesitate he reconsidered in-direction, a principle he'd abandoned, temporarily. "Excuse me for asking, I'll go home and write you a letter." She was still frowning as she rummaged through the packaged soups.

"They always have a shitload of onion and mushroom but never the ones I want. Who buys up all the spring vegetable and the garden vegetable? It's those fucking health freaks!" And turning back to face him: "Sal's not working tonight, he pulled day shift for himself the rest of this month." And maybe because he couldn't keep his mouth from slackening? "But come down anyway and have some coffee with us, maybe there's a good movie on, you can hold Nikky's hand on the couch." Why did she enjoy needling him? From the security of his own stoop, resting his groceries, he offered Carbone a cigarette and asked him point-blank. "Yeah, I seen him around. Some. Kinda guy you'd always bump into, so I never paid no attention to him. His clothes always looked like he slept in them."

Watching Carbone's lip curl, the kid decided his risk was small. "Did anybody ever get close with him—I mean, hang around with him, know him real well?"

Carbone scraped at a stain the kid couldn't see, then traced the knife crease in his cord pants with his thumbnail and forefinger. "Who you working for?" His grin, to deprecate, didn't reassure the kid.

"She was on my caseload, the one he killed. In fact, the day before was my day in the field but I skipped her, she didn't need checking up on. Though usually she was my first stop, she made good coffee." Actually she always made instant coffee, very weak. "So I've been thinking about writing something about it—about her—and about him. It's the first public thing that ever happened I feel close to."

Sometimes I say: "Well, maybe he'll make supervisor if he stays on another two years, or even another year now, the way they're losing people. But he's not the career type." Sometimes I just shrug: "Well, I wouldn't say he likes it, but he's learning a lot. But it's wearing, it drains him, sometimes he comes home so beat he can't even talk about what he's seen." It depends on who's asking. Why should I have to defend him, nobody expects anything from him any more! Sometimes I get exasperated and snap their heads off. "What else should he do, edit dictionaries? Go back to grad school? Or teach? More real problems cross his desk in a day than you see in a year! And besides he doesn't talk to me about what he's really into, for all I know he's writing the great American novel." When they don't laugh I realize they're actually worried he might outflank them.

Would he be flattered? They saw none of his friends, who stopped being curious soon after he stopped phoning; it takes barely six months to forget a phone number and he was never the kind you called up casually, to chat with. It's a big city, he whistled, savoring the sense of his demise, sinking into the street world. But avoided the uptown cinemas and the few bars he guessed they still patronized. Laurie's crowd didn't count, he sniffed at their expensive linen, leched after their women, luckily there'd never been overlaps. Of course he wouldn't tell her, tool for humiliation if it didn't work out. Evidence. He recopied his notes, added descriptions of all the children. And Thomas. Stole her folder, those originals he could risk keeping and Xeroxes of records he stamped CLOSED and shipped upstairs. He wanted photographs, not necessarily her wedding picture taped onto the oval mirror of her dresser, but at least one with some of the children, snapshots. "Just some background stuff," he mumbled to Laurie once, she'd surprised him shuffling his index cards, the few clippings neatly pasted. Locked them into his desk drawer.

LAURIE *I always have this same dream about reading how my mother died in a plane crash, even after I wake up it never surprises me, I guess way inside I think that's what newspapers are for. Three winters ago I saw this squib about a Cape patrolman drowned trying to rescue a capsized fisherman, stared at his name in the smudgy print till the letters blurred and I couldn't focus. We rented the beach cottage beside his saltbox for five straight summers. I played with his kids, his youngest boy nibbled my breasts under my wet suit when we sand-wrestled, he was too short for me but accidentally I'd run my fingers over the smooth olive skin of his thighs. His father had blond tangled curls matting his chest; bowlegged he'd shout his kids in to dinner from his back steps like a tribal chief, his little girl squalled when he tossed her. Naturally she played tomboy, pummeled his broad back and practiced spitting through her front teeth at the rest of us. He gave me rides into town in his police car so I could parade the beach in my tight white jeans. "Now don't you be causing no trouble with all them hot bloods!" he'd shout after me, and I'd turn to wave goodbye, flushed but pleased, I knew what he was seeing. Or thought I did. And if he'd moved, once, touched my hand before I could open my door or fingered my hair with his huge callused fingers? I cried for almost an hour, fresh wave would choke me long after I thought I'd finished, and yet I never heard his name, only read it in the paper, we always called him Mister.*

Almost closing time, watching the old man wind up his awning, gnarled hands spinning his oiled crank in a hesitant circle, he sucked his finger, waiting. The old man hobbled

62

back into his store and arrested, one by one, the three imitation-leather-topped stools the kid had spun into motion, then edged behind the counter to wipe the already clean marble top with a damp dishcloth. "Lissen I'm gonna close up soon." So the kid ordered another lemon ice, his third. "But everybody says you knew him better than anybody else. Certainly enough to talk to."

Resigned shrug but a hint of anger, tamping the ice with his scoop, honest value, hands no longer aware of their motions overfill the cup. Could just as well pass off a false bottom on me, he knows he doesn't have to bother with my money's worth. At least not in lemon ice. I'd lay something on him if I knew the right way. "He's always come in here. Sometimes a candy bar, sometimes a Coke, once in a while maybe a pack cigars. What's he gonna say? I say hello, he says hello. Maybe it's a hot day I say it's hot he says yeah, it's hot. Same thing in winter. He's not the kinda guy shoots his mouth off. Maybe once or twice he complains about his leg. Otherwise he keep his mouth shut, he don't push himself on people. Besides which we weren't related."

So the kid avoids the hand extending his cup of lemon ice, but the old man sets the cup on the counter and turns away to replace the cover of the lemon ice carton, pounds its edges closed and lowers it into its freezer well. "Look I'm sorry I gotta close up now." His wife doesn't trouble to dissemble, tries to catch the kid's eye to glare at him. "It's already twenty past and we gotta eat quick, we got a meeting at the church to go to." Apologetic mumble, actually it was Bingo and just last week he was three cards away from Giordano's mother-in-law who keeled over and passed away right there on the

63

floor, she needed only one more number to fill her bottom line. Drained but hospitable, twenty years behind his own counter, the secret of Manhattan's finest Italian ice would die with him, lately his wife had begun to fear they'd never see Florida although he'd made all the deposits. The kid sucked noisily at his ice. "You were in the club when he finally got back from the war. De Marco told me you were the only one who remembered what his girl looked like. And you were there the day he fell off the ladder and ruined his knee."

Successive blinks seemed to tug his eyes back at the corners, chasing a shadow through torn pages, fading scrapbook photographs. "We don't need your lousy fifteen cents, get the hell outa here now and let us close up." Wife pushed an angry broom across worn floorboards, menacing the kid's sandals with a thin wedge of dust; suddenly he was ashamed of his filthy toenails. "You're working for some crummy paper, you just want dirt. We told the police all anybody's gonna know, and we don't owe you nothing. And anyway you're wasting your time. He was only a drunk that killed a nigger."

SAL *One time I thought he was gonna call me by name. Two of the boys was taking him downtown for his arraignment, I let them into the cage. "Why they lock me up?"*

"Lock you up?" I thought maybe he meant in the van, the way they brought him in. "You go down in a regular police car, they won't lock you up." Kept staring at me till I began to feel I'd let him down. "Dutch, I'm trying to help but I don't know what you mean." Jangled his cuffs at me, shook his clamped wrists. "These."

"Oh, that! Doesn't mean anything, Dutch. Just a formality. They

64

put the cuffs on everybody who goes downtown." Which wasn't strictly true, we put them on anybody we think needs them. Manslaughter and up we put them on without thinking, but it ain't an ironclad requirement. I woulda skipped it with Dutch but they'd already cuffed him, I didn't like contradicting the boys. "It don't mean anything."

"Where they take me?"

"To court. For your arraignment." Like telling him for his Bar Mitzvah. "A lawyer'll be there standing up for you, the Counselor got you one. It's just a formality—they'll read the charges against you, and ask you how you plead. The lawyer'll handle the whole thing."

Maybe Hanratty was wrong, maybe he won't turn out to be a zombie. Guys like him take a long time working something outa their system, and it ain't that easy killing anybody, even a nigger. The boys could see he still had something to say so they didn't rush him, nobody pushed him around the whole time he was at the precinct.

"In front of the Judge, I have to wear these?"

Farillo beat me to it. "We'll make an exception," he says, unlocks the cuffs and slips them off Dutch's wrists. He nodded, closest I ever seen him get to saying thank you.

65

Aluminum of the examining table cold on his bare ass, Matto, his soggy pants rolled over his swollen knee and then tugged off by a disdainful nurse, waits. Needle, when it finally plunged, seared him: "Ai! Aii!" His fists clamped the thin table edge so tightly his knuckles showed white, but still his right leg bucked as his knee locked, straining to expel the needle point. His lower leg kicked out again and the needle slipped through the younger doctor's tentative fingers, slid down the puffy mound of kneecap and dropped to the floor. Matto was relieved it hadn't shattered. His blood followed it.

"Nurse!" Older doctor, harsh, impatient. Another needle quickly sterilized. "And the knee, please."

He didn't feel the blood ooze, matting his knee, staining (he discovered that evening) his socks after trickling through the thick hair of his lower leg, thin red paste clotted with egg-white pulp. His knee was burning. "Ice, ice!" he begged. Nurse's cotton pads soaked as she sopped, soft pats, skin subsiding like dough under her practiced fingers only to puff and bulge again as she discarded her stained pads. Matto couldn't see her wrinkle her nose.

"Better try it again!" from the older doctor. "I've had the same trouble with those knees. Tricky business. Too deep and you're through the impacted area, too shallow and there's not enough tissue lodgment to withstand the drainage pressure. Maybe," shuffle of footsteps across the shiny floor, "if you just try it on the slant, like that—there, that's it! Just at the base of that protrusion. There! Good! That looks like it. Just bunch that flesh a little—nurse! Hold his leg steady! Now—jab!"

67

Matto's teeth locked, clamping his lower lip, but he couldn't choke off his whimpers.

"Quiet!"

"I—I think it's lodged now," the younger doctor whispered. "Can we get the clamp on? Ah—good. Good work. Thank you, nurse. Now if you could just keep an eye on the drainage?"

First trickles of pus oozed into the pan, but Matto couldn't open his eyes to see both doctors straighten, square their shoulders as the yellowish-white fluid, intestine color, flowed through colorless tubing to spill into the nurse's enameled tray. Matto uncurled his fingers. *Ice. Freeze it and chip out the bad pieces and sew me a new knee, pins and wire, like Dominic's jaw. Sew it up, patch a new net with fisherman's cord, throw any crab overboard smaller than five fingers, even when they crack their claws on your pole.*

"Bend it." A pause. "Bend that knee!"

Matto's eyelids waver, he fights for focus, wheels dizzily back from the Jersey beach where he and Joey and Mike raced three girls in one-piece bathing suits across wet sand to the water's edge, green and orange beach ball contriving to elude them, out into deeper water, over his head, fear cramping his stomach as he dog-paddled toward the ball. Bottom of the boat they rented crawling with crabs, stalks and claws pawing their legs as the crabs slid, clinking, as waves rocked them, bushel barrels overflowing with blue-black shells and gesticulating feelers till they felt trapped in an ark of crabs and still kept pulling up more. Two baskets tipped over and the

68

crabs reached the fish heads, all their extra bait, they balanced on the crossboards to preserve their legs from nips and bites already beginning to swell. Finally they jumped into the choppy sea and swam to shore, abandoning the boat, derelict graveyard for hundreds of crabs unable to crawl up its wet sloping sides to flop back into the sea—

"Bend that knee. Bend it! Wake up, you!"

His cheekbone swollen, distorting the right side of his face and twisting his gray scrubby mustache, the older doctor glares at Matto. "Bend it, dammit, can't you hear?" Flush mottling his forehead, splotched skin. Patchy. "Nurse, bend that knee. Either he can't understand English or he's an idiot."

"Fuck you," Matto grunts. "Goddam butcher."

Sharp sucking intake of breath and diffident, crisp footsteps as the nurse edges between Matto and the stooping younger doctor. A gentle pressure down and reluctantly, the knee flexes, Matto whimpers as the needle rips tissue. Her hands relax, his lower leg floats upward as his muscles strain to articulate the cap, sag and then expand. "Again!" And again Matto whimpers, stares at the vibrating plunger, wills to eject it, force its point up through the layers of tissue to clatter into the tray already stained with his blood and pus. "Again, nurse. Articulate it." Bent so her reddish curls under her starched cap are level with Matto's crotch, the nurse works his leg like a pump handle, forcing out the thick fluid. Matto's mumble a counterpoint. "Fucking butcher. Butcher. Butcher."

"Ignore it. Just ignore it." Perhaps because the younger doctor glanced up, licked his lips, considered a tentative

69

protest? Or disclaimer? Stiff, shoulders forced back,
the older doctor continued his inspection of the trickle of
yellow fluid.

The younger doctor wriggles his foot and then taps his toe
repeatedly against the cross-brace of the examining table.
"It looks as if it's—is that the worst of it?"

"A little longer. First real flow of blood will clear it. That's
fine, nurse. That's very good. Just a little more now."

"Aah." Shivers. His leg dangles, no longer flexed.

"Whew! That's better. Angry-looking knee." Younger doctor
wiped his brow and then his lower lip, ran his fingers over
his stubbled chin, remembering he'd forgotten to shave and
wondered whether the older man had noticed. And minded.
"Caught it earlier, might've brought it down with Cortisone,
I guess. Certainly a good chance. But now that tissue's so
inflamed—"

"Neglected it. Ignored it till he couldn't move, hoping if
he let it alone it might get better. Either they come running
in here every time they get a twinge or they don't come in till
it's too late. When did you first hurt that knee?"

"It's all right now," the nurse was whispering, light fingertaps
on his forearm. "It's all right now, it's all over, all I have to do
is bandage it up and that won't hurt, you can open your eyes
now."

Matto opened his eyes.

The older doctor, leaning against the file cabinet. "How long
ago did you first hurt that knee?"

70

"First?" Matto stared at the floor and then his toes. "Long time ago." Plank borrowed from Nick's brother-in-law stretched between two ladders, Maria's rickety old wooden stepladder and the new metal one Herman contributed to the club. Matto pushing dust off the ceiling with rollers, splotting and covering the dust he can't dislodge with a thick coating of white paint which clotted his hair, speckled his forehead, even his eyelids were coated. "Why don't you wear a cap, you donkey? I'll need a whole bottle of turpentine just for your hair, I'll get sick from the smell of it." Turning to smile at Maria he heard fibers snap, lurched as the plank swayed, buckled, can flipped paint in a white spiral which coated counter and window, his right arm grabbed for the can's sturdy handle, dubious anchor, as he fell.

"His chart shows treatment going back to 1957. For that knee." The nurse, hesitantly, crouching to ease a gauze pad onto the knee and then wind a bandage round. "Mostly for the cartilage."

"Yes. Well, we'll have to X-ray that, I'm afraid." Younger doctor blinking at Matto as the nurse secured the gauze wrapping, criss-crossing the tape which would anchor the bandage and steady the knee. "When the inflammation's down a bit more. Might be some of the cap damaged, as well as all that tissue bruised. And the cartilage is probably torn. Can't tell without an X-ray. You'll have to make another appointment."

Over her shoulder, quick glance at the older doctor who sniffed, contemptuous. "We don't work on appointments here," the nurse mumbled, apologetic. "All he has to do is

71

come to Out-Patients, they'll send him for his X-ray. As long as it's marked on his chart.''

Resting his palms against the damp table, back crooked forward, Matto scraped the tip of his tongue across the back of his teeth as his knee began to throb again. "Oh, I—I wasn't told that," the younger doctor muttered. "Well, in that case, we'll need to see you in—I guess, about a week, a week should do it. A week seem about right to you, for that inflammation to go down?" Evasive glance at the older doctor, pretending absorption in Matto's chart. "And you'd better stay off that— keep off your feet as much as possible. In bed most of the day, don't walk until there's no pain left. Are you off work? Or can you take sick leave?"

"No."

"You can't take sick leave?"

Matto waited. Then he shook his head.

"Oh. Well at least stay off your feet. Rest that leg as much as you can. It'll be dangerous to put any strain on that knee. What kind of work do you do?"

"Load trucks."

"Oh. I see." Again the younger doctor peeked over his shoulder. "Well, ah, I guess in that line of work you—couldn't you collect unemployment? Just for a couple of weeks? Or call in sick, tell them what happened to you? We can give you a certificate if you want one."

"No unemployment. No disability. No sick leave. Dollar an hour, no insurance." Matto lifted his head, his knee throbbed.

"Day labor. Donkey work. Get to agency eight thirty every morning, stand in line for work. Ten per cent commission. Once in a while free coffee. I stay home, nobody cares. Hospital pay me to stay home?"

The nurse, rolling up Matto's soggy trousers so she could slide them over his knee, swathed now in a massive white guard, measured the older doctor's snort and waited through the pause which meant he was forming, word by word, a devastating retort as he tapped Matto's chart. Renowned throughout Orthopedics for his wit, he was reputed to have driven at least two clumsy nurses to tears. The younger doctor fumbled his jacket buttons and then stared down at his fingers as if he'd expected a more elegant interlacing. But the older doctor found, after consideration, nothing satisfying to say, set Matto's folder on the nurse's table and turned to the door.

"Well, if you really have to work, you'll need some support for that knee. It's still risky to use it at all, but at least you should have a pair of crutches. You might even be able to prop yourself up, once in a while, as you're working. Nurse, how do we get him a pair of crutches?"

"He can get by with a cane." Sharply, from the door, before the nurse could begin to explain requisition procedure.

"But—I mean—with that degree of inflammation, especially if he can't afford to take off work, I'd have thought that at least—" The older doctor never bothered to glance at Matto. "He's had two pairs of crutches and three canes allocated since 1957. Check his records. Nurse, requisition him a cane to borrow, so he can get home. Make sure it's marked *on loan*. Explain to him that if he doesn't return it when he comes back

73

next week, he won't get his knee X-rayed. That Irish woman with the bursitis in her shoulder's already been sent in?"

He pushed through the cubicle's swinging door. Younger doctor, still wagging his head, turned to Matto. "Well, make sure and take care of that leg. Don't work any harder than you have to. And I'll see you next week." A nod and a grimace Matto didn't see and the younger doctor pushed through the door, hurrying after the taller figure disappearing into another cubicle. "You can get into these yourself, can't you?" Nurse handed Matto his damp bunched trousers, retreated to her charts to write and tear off a requisition slip. "You don't have those canes any more, do you?" As Matto shook his head, trying to grope his left foot into its trouser leg, crouching to dangle the trousers to save bending his knee, she decided she couldn't risk ordering crutches, no way to alter what Supply would stamp in his records, she could brazen it past the younger one but if the other one ever checked out her records there'd be hell to pay. And he just might, she thought, he's the type who remembers. "You just take this downstairs, third window on the left of the elevators, it says Supplies over the window. You hand it to the girl there, she'll give you a cane. Just keep it and use it, you don't have to bring it back. And don't mind what that doctor says," she whispered. "He's a sour man, he takes it out on everybody, nobody likes him. He's leaving soon." She smiled as she handed the slip over, but both Matto's hands were suspending his trousers, so she set the slip beside him, thinking that canes cost maybe forty-five cents apiece the way the hospital bought them, thousands at a time. In the cubicle across the hall, empty because a student nurse had misdirected the Irish woman with

74

bursitis in her shoulder, the older doctor yawned, elaborately. "They sell everything they can get their hands on. You'd have been requisitioning those crutches straight to a pawnshop." Later that night, after discussing the incident in bed with his wife, the younger doctor decided what he should have said.

*Carson left the clipping on my desk, outlined in red. How the
hell does she remember all the names on my caseload?*

*I couldn't stay at my desk. Two cops on duty, stopping
everybody going into the building, one of them told me the
kids had disappeared. When I finally got back to the office
I called the precinct. "Missing without a trace." I scrawled it
across the kids' pages, wrote CASE CLOSED on the lip
of her folder. My first entry was late October 1963, I'd seen
her five times.*

10/22/63

Mrs. Eliza Wilson called, ADC1471-837. OAA refuses to
answer queries about her mother's whereabouts, last records
at nursing home two years old.

*Carson tossed the note on my desk. "Tell her we're not
running a Missing Persons bureau." Curious, I climbed her
stairs, only a month short of my required statutory visit, my
grandfather died in a nursing home where embittered men
locked themselves in the toilets on visiting days. "Come on in,"
she shouted from the kitchen, sorting Corinna's baby clothes
still stiff from the clothesline, "door's open, it's never closed.
Just keep following the sound." I could smell the bleach on
her hands. "I used to visit her every Sunday, right after
church I'd take the bus, but then I got sick and after that
Thomas started coming by, and with one thing after another,
time went by. Now when I call they tell me they got no
records on her. And here I visited her in the same place every
Sunday for three years and they got no records? But I can't
get nothing outa them, every time they told me they couldn't*

77

help I'd ask them, well what should I do? They'd wait for a long time and then they hang up." When I promised her I'd find out, she nodded. "You probably will. I guess I'm lucky I'm on the State, otherwise I wouldn't have nobody white to turn to."

Only apartment on my whole caseload I could relax in. "How many investigators you had?" I asked her once. She shook her head. "I never counted. First one was one too many. Couple were real bastards, hated my guts and said so. And a couple more never showed up, never could find them when you needed something. So you ain't bad. You don't know much, and it seems like you learn slow, but you don't mind talking, and you ain't asked for more than coffee. Yet."

Not that I had principled objections. Just felt inept, too much to handle. Her slow body heaving up off her chair to scoop Claudie into the bathroom. Stared at her mountainous breasts, placid beneath her housecoat while I sipped her coffee, thinking I'd probably smother. So I guess Thomas bothered me. He was just there too often. One morning I wanted a cup of her coffee and some easy chatter to put the best possible face on the rest of my day. Thomas was in his shorts, I snapped before I thought. "What the hell are you doing here, you trying to get me fired?" Thomas propped his bare feet on her rickety table. "Now why the hell should I care whether you get fired or not?" He was right, in retrospect I decided, but then I wanted to kick his chair out from under him. "Look, if I get fired on account of you, you might not wind up in jail but she'd damn sure lose her grant. I've seen you here three times now and covered for you each time, there's a state law not only makes you liable for the kids but says you can be

78

arrested just for sitting here. You probably didn't even watch out for yourself when you came in, the whole building might know you're here."

"You just worry 'bout what you write in that little black book, I'll worry about the neighbors. She ever gets cut off, I'll know how to say thanks."

"Thomas, hush up. Just you hush up." And turned to me. "How come you here so early this morning? You decide to do a little checking up on your own?"

I shook my head. "No, I wasn't trying to check up. Today's my day in the field. I decided to start here."
"Your day in the what?" she said. Thomas just snorted.

Memo to DW:
In response to your form 82Y of 10/22. Mrs. A. Saunders deceased 8/15/62, Mendelsohn Branch, NY State OA Shelter. Interred in state grounds, LI Cemetery by State Order #44H-517. No marker.

I kept it for eight days, debated mailing it to her. Guilt finally forced me up her stairs. I set it on her table and just shook my head when she asked me, she set her iron to rest on her radiator and walked over to read it.

"I'm sorry."

She tapped the memo with a discolored nail. "Momma was a proud woman, and yet she always said they'd bury her in the Potter's Field." She washed her hands with the kosher soap she claimed she bought because Jews always get their money's

79

worth, wiped them slowly on a faded dishtowel, smoothed out the letter's creases and folded it into Linda's Bible. Then she eased herself into her kitchen chair and rocked on its hind legs, nodding. I coughed and cleared my throat, wanting to go. "After my daddy went up North he sent back money every month so my momma could board us while she cooked for my aunt in her restaurant. When she had enough money saved up she carted us all North, only to find my daddy shacked up with another woman. And moved right in. After a month the other woman left and after six months my daddy left. You can get out now," she said. "You did what you said. I'm 'bout to cry, there ain't nothing you can do about it, and no need to be watching."

After I cleared up her records and buried her file I roamed her streets. Stray details now useless, that laundromat I never noticed before she must've used for her heavy loads. Attendant shook his head, ancient machines grinding. "Nobody leaves their name here, just their wash." The guy in the pocket bodega winked at me. "Big woman with good boobs, no? Very touchy! She stopped her kids coming in here because she thought I padded the tab. Maybe once or twice, but when I realized she was particular I treated her right. She just never realized how much candy those kids could eat."

I walked past the beauty parlor but didn't have the guts, and the other stores she might've used seemed too peripheral. The kids were gone, one of a hundred possible relatives had spirited them uptown or across the river, over to Jersey, down to Philadelphia or Baltimore, west as far as Chicago. "Look, wait a second, I was Mrs. Wilson's investigator, the man from the Welfare, from the State," I shouted. She didn't want

*to stop. Downstairs neighbor, seen me on the stairs enough
to remember me but wanted to forget me now, pressing against
her stomach something tightly wrapped in thick brown paper
and heavy gray twine. "All I'm trying to do is find out what
happened to the kids—they still got money due to them from
the State."*

*Reluctantly she set her parcel on a garbage-can lid. "Every-
body wants to know. What makes them kids so damn important
all of a sudden? Police wants to know, Child Care wants to
know, now you want to know. I'll tell you what I told them,
sister-in-law took those kids up to the Bronx. If I knew her
name I wouldn't tell you."*

That left Thomas.

*This morning I told Carson: "You'd only laugh at me."
"Probably," Carson nodded, "but if you're already prepared,
it won't hurt so bad. Sit down and tell me about it."*

*"I need a couple of days. Two at the most. I need to see a
couple of people involved in Mrs. Wilson's case. Nothing
specific. And on my own time. If you cover for me for two
days, I'll do my reports at home."*

*"Forget it. Just catch up by the end of the week. If
you're headed uptown, stay away from the Center, they'll
think you're part of some special investigative unit.
See you."*

*Prophetic as usual. I hated uptown. I had one address for
Thomas, phone number really, bar and pool hall he gave me
"in case something happens to the kids." Claudie and Corinne
were his. I hated uptown. Nobody I know even goes to the*

Apollo any more. Naturally the bar was a mile from the subway, I'd taken the wrong line. Zigzagged through tenement blocks, my eyes fixed on the next few squares of sidewalk, side-stepping the hordes of kids scampering through the streets but prickling under the stares their elders gave me as they sat fanning themselves on wooden folding chairs on their stoops and shop doorways. A storefront church threatened to spill its congregation into the street so I circled it, then past another storefront stained like a frosted Victorian bathroom window, I didn't stop to read which brotherhood sang. Finally I reached the Avenue.

I knew if I started to hesitate I'd never go on, so I shoved the door open but it banged too loudly behind me, everybody looked up. Or seemed to. "What you want?" I heard, but couldn't locate the speaker, besides I had no answer. He sat in the back, at a table by himself in the shadows without a drink, watching a bald man with massively hunched shoulders circle his table with a short but fluid stroke. "Thomas," I said. He nodded, motioned me to the seat beside him. I sat down and then pushed my chair back, banging my shin on the table's crosspiece. "I'll buy you a drink." Two bourbons, a good strong Kentucky. I knew what he liked, with ginger ale for chasers, I would've bought him a cigar just to be allowed to sit but he might've asked what I thought I was celebrating. He sipped at the thick rim. So I sipped at mine.

"I was gonna call you for money for the undertaker. But her brother kept claiming he'd cover it all. He's high-handed, can't stomach me, thinks I'm trash, thinks I held Liza down. We've tangled before. That's why I never showed up at the funeral."

82

We sat. I toyed with my drink, sipping as slowly as I could, but I was still finished long before he took his second sip. I wondered if he'd ever known her age. "I checked back in her records—she was only thirty-seven. I never realized she was that young."

Some moments later he shifted his weight and his chair creaked. "I started remembering how long we'd been seeing each other. I actually ran into her in the old emergency ward down in that hospital near the Slip. She had one of her kids wrapped up in a blanket, some damn fool had just split the side of my head open with a chair. One of them doctors tried to give her a hard time and she just lit out after him, followed him right through the doors into his ward, yelling she'd take the place apart until they tended to her daughter. They did. Some kind of fever. I made my mind up right then I wanted to see that woman, got one of the brothers on the ward to find out her address for me. That was four, maybe even five years ago."

"She told me the story once. It was Melinda and she was coming down with some kind of septic fever, she thought Melinda was dying. And then the doctor tried to tell her it wasn't really an emergency and she should come back in the morning or go to a private doctor, at two o'clock after she'd already woken Mrs. Turner to watch the rest of the kids and hitched a ride from a milk truck down to the Slip."

"You got a good memory," Thomas said, "and I'm grateful for the bourbon, but why don't you get the hell outa here? There's all kinda ways of doing the man's work"

Angie had Lawrence Welk on when he knocked, he could hear the wheezy accordian spilling polka music through her hollow door. She slid the safety latch back, why bother to double-lock your door with a cop in your kitchen? "You're just in time," she grinned up at him, housecoat open on a pale blue slip, "we're still working on our second cup of coffee." Nikky was jabbing a pair of Angie's old shoes with a broken scissors and the screen was bellying Welk's grin at the bulge of the tube and then tumbling it in a slow floating motion, just as the top of Welk's head disappeared his torso would drift into view. "Sit down, I'll pour you a cup. It's still hot."

A nod toward Sal, and an answering glower. I wouldn't be gracious either, in your shoes, the kid thought. "You back on day shift again?" Only a grunt for response. "Sit down," Angie said. "We were just talking about Markowitz, the stingy bastard, trying to figure out how we could maneuver him into air-conditioning the whole building."

"Momma, I wanna change it, can I change it?" Nikky hollered.

Eased into his seat, vinyl chair covering already sticky against his jeans. "I walked down by the river today, see if I could get away from the heat a little. Your people really cruise those piers. Seemed like every time I stopped near a row of trailer trucks there was a squad car slowing down to watch me. Those trucks get boosted a lot?"

Another shrug. And reluctantly: "I dunno. It ain't my division." And after a pause: "There's a special pier security squad, it mighta been their cars. And most of the shipping companies pay for their own private patrols, they got radio hook-ups from inside."

85

"Nope. These were straight squad cars. Fourth Precinct, not Safety Division." A decent response, given Sal's standards, why push it? "Couple of them who stopped to watch me looked just about ready to call me over. Guess if I'd been black they wouldn't have hesitated."

"They're just doing their job." Sal set his cup down and tipped his stool back. "Besides if you was colored you probably wouldn't be down there in the first place, you might have something better to do. It's small pickings down there unless you're organized. Happens at night, whole trailers through the tunnel to Jersey where they get unloaded, the stuff they're carrying gets split up. They mighta thought you were a spotter, trying to figure out what's inside each trailer. Most times the gangs get advance word but sometimes they use people spotting the loads, figuring out which trailers are heavy and what they're carrying."

"I thought it wasn't your division."

"Now look, don't start that shit again. The two of you don't spend five minutes together without looking for a fight, you're worse than a coupla women! We were spending a quiet Saturday night before you came in; if you can't sit and talk decent, go in and watch TV with Nikky." Noticing she didn't suggest getting out, the kid was reassured. "You're right. I always come in with a chip on my shoulder, whenever Sal's around. But it's not my imagination that I see more cops every day. Makes me jumpy."

"Momma I wanna change it, I don't like that silly man and the picture won't hold still!"

86

"Well," Sal said reluctantly, stretching to scratch the back of his neck, "you gotta remember it's summertime already, the whole city's jumpy. After last summer you can't tell what's gonna happen, the least little spark and we got people in the streets which is what we got the strictest orders to prevent. By any means necessary. The boys at City Hall have been very clear, we get through this summer without any incidents uptown or across the river and we just might have pretty smooth sailing, come bargaining time in October. But anything breaks out and the shit hits the fan for us."

"This city'll never survive a policemen's strike," Angie said.

"You can't stop a riot with heavier surveillance," the kid said. "You're just helping to heat things up.

"I don't give a fuck if a goddam riot breaks out in five or six spots all over the city, all they'll do is burn down some building shoulda been torn down years ago, wipe out some crummy Jew stores been stealing nickels and dimes outa their crummy neighborhoods. Who gives a fuck? If it was up to me I'd give them half the city and never send a cruiser in. They could hustle all the dope they wanted and bump each other off in broad daylight."

"I wanna change it, I wanna change it!" Nikky screamed. "Momma, momma, I wanna change it, I wanna change it now!"

Angie scraped the kid's fly with her hand and then her thigh as she edged around the kitchen table only because the kitchen was so cramped since she'd moved the refrigerator. Nikky

87

would begin to pound the floor with her fists and then her feet and finally with the already scarred ridge of her forehead, the last bout with Angie cost three stitches and an injection before she stopped screaming. "It'll come to that," the kid said without conviction from somewhere behind her housecoat as she squirmed past him; he debated snaking a careful hand under her slip. "One of these days you'll find yourself behind a barricade with your pistol cocked, wondering whether there's enough of you to hold out."

"And when that fine day comes," Sal said, "I'll take my chances with the rest of the boys on the force. But just where will you be?"

ANGIE   *I walked out on them, switched the goddam set to another channel and stroked Nikky's head and played with her curls and the tickly spots behind her ears till I had her giggling. Sometimes I just wanted Sal to smash the kid's head through the kitchen cabinet. But it was me after all invited him down, and if I wasn't going to kick him out I couldn't just sit there and let them argue, neither one was having much fun. So I shoved myself up off my ass and marched back in. "Lissen," I said to the kid. "Sal says you been scouting the neighborhood trying to pick up more tidbits on Matto. How come you never asked me? I went with Al the grocery manager during the whole winter Matto was working nights at the supermarket. The winter before the Polack squealed."*

And she couldn't remember what she'd never been told. Al was one of the few who never talked, even afterwards. The rest of the crew swore they kept their mouths shut but actually boasted all over the neighborhood, flashed their money and spread it around, the only time they were careful was when they broke in somebody new. They

88

worked Matto's ass off for months, barely talking to him, isolating him in the coffee breaks but checking his order sheets and prices like they had shares in the company. Matto tried to please but couldn't crack their reserve; bewildered, he fumbled out a plea for explanation. "We're watching you, that's all you need to know. This here's an elite crew, nobody in the city works as tight as we do."

When one of their regulars got transferred uptown they had to decide overnight whether to take him in or cut their take. They took him in, congratulated him on having survived his probation, pleased with themselves at their foresight, a new man and a painless transition. But they watched every flicker of his eyelids as Al explained how their system worked. The take was worth $200 a night per person easy, if Matto had pleaded cold feet they'd have considered getting rid of him. But Matto never even measured the risk, whatever they did was fine with him, and if he came home every Friday with triple his paycheck in his pocket? Aunt Carrie could always use a little extra.

They had it easy. Night shift started at ten p.m.; by one, after the cigarette breaks, several cups of coffee, and finally a huge meal—frozen steaks from the griddle, fried onions, melted cheese, torpedo rolls, gallons of Coke—they had already finished most of their eight-hour quota. After another round of coffee with maybe a beer or a nip from a flask somebody remembered to bring in, they settled down for a nap; nobody else would sleep in the produce warehouse but Matto was used to dampness, shipboard molded his clothes and rotted his collars, he spread heavy burlap potato sacks into a dusty quilting and squirmed into a lumpy sleep. Between two thirty and three o'clock Voto's unmarked pick-up pulled up to the loading platform and beeped, softly, before parking next to one of the loaded trailers, Al stayed awake to guide him in. Nobody bothered to tell Matto how

89

much of his night's work went into the Teamster treasury, not that he would've begrudged it. But Al must've known their time was limited, yearly inventory would show so big a gap between total intake and volume, ten trailer trucks wouldn't restore the balance, what was he figuring on? Every night after three trips in Voto's pick-up had unloaded a couple thousand dollars worth of name-brand canned goods at Voto's warehouse, they divided up the same way, one share for everybody. Voto paid a flat 40 per cent off current store prices, and Al stood with the regulation warehouse list, checking off each carton, he even gave Voto reductions on damaged cartons and dented cans, though the crew was careful to hold the damage down, their own money at stake. Voto added another 40 per cent for himself when he sold off the cartons to dozens of neighborhood merchants who charged their customers a penny or two more per can than the supermarket price and pocketed a handsome 20 per cent instead of their usual 4 per cent, which barely covered overhead. Top speed two or three nights a week, they put maybe $350 to $500 extra in their pockets, tax-free. During those six months of night work Matto banked over $5,000.

Until the Polack squealed. Next to Al, he'd worked the warehouse the longest, but he never complained, often volunteered to cook the steaks and always remembered that Matto liked his medium, with the fat burned. His cans always displayed the store's neatest prices, stamped square into the center and never smudged; cashiers always knew the aisles he'd worked the night before. Al guessed it was some whim of his wife's he'd forgotten about till punch-out time. Maybe she was pregnant, maybe she nagged him, maybe it was something he always promised to bring home and then forgot and this time he decided he wouldn't come home empty-handed. How much difference could three little cans of mushrooms shoved into his coat sleeves make,

90

after hundreds of thousands of dollars already untrucked and sold off?
A small fortune, as it turned out, shot, for the whole crew. Matto was
fumbling with the oversize top button of his new mackinaw as the
Polack ambled out of the aisles and headed for the door and the park-
ing lot. "Hold it a minute, buddy." Store detective, shorter than
Matto. "New policy, we're checking all the staff this week. Mind if
I pat you down? It's only routine."

Al figured afterwards the detective probably spotted the Polack, no-
body knew he was in the store so the Polack wouldn't have bothered
to be careful. "Okay, buddy," the store detective said, he'd reached up
into the Polack's armpits to extract the three tiny cans of mushrooms.
"I guess we better go see the manager." One of us should've stopped
him, Al said afterwards, but I never imagined he'd panic. The worst
he'd have gotten was a week in the manager's doghouse and we'd still
be working. The night crew gradually drifted together to stare through
the frosted glass at the indistinct blur of the manager's face as he
listened to the Polack. Al said he wanted to run but the cruiser from
the precinct had already showed up to wait for the bank to deliver the
sacks of coins and bills for the cashiers' tills. The manager kept clear-
ing his throat. "Publicity's what we don't want, otherwise you boys
would already be down at the precinct. But this kind of thing always
pushes sales down, once it gets out; somehow people decide there's
something fishy going on and feel more comfortable shopping else-
where. So I think we'll probably decide to keep this one quiet, at
least until I check with the head office. But don't think you're getting
a break. We can prefer charges against you any time we want. And
I wouldn't try working for anybody's grocery department or ware-
house again. I'll make sure the word gets around." It did. After Al's
convertible was impounded, and Matto's and Jeff's bank accounts
frozen and seized, and the lump payment received from Voto after

*his lawyers read the night crew's signed statements which the man-
ager and the police had demanded, the manager recouped enough of
his loss to bring his yearly gross figures under the 5 per cent margin
allowed him on the books for losses through theft and accidental destruction.*

SAL   *I knew the kid was bad news first morning I met him, sipping
Angie's coffee. Nobody had to draw me a map. Angie grinned and
pointed a finger at his mop of hair, it was so matted he couldn't stand
to put a comb through it until after his coffee. Sensitive kid.*

*After he went downstairs once he was sure his wife was gone,
Angie tried to explain but I cut her off. We weren't kids any more, I
been around long enough to know what trouble looks like when it's
sitting in your kitchen. When I got back to the precinct I looked him
up, but we didn't have anything on him except one complaint from
his downstairs neighbors about a noisy party. At least he kept his
nose clean.*

*He got on my ass. Any kid with a college degree could walk into
Welfare and knock down an investigator's job at a hundred a week,
Department was dying for staff, but he hadda pretend he was on a
mission! He started lecturing me one morning and I got pissed off, I
been in and out of tenements for forty-five years. "Lissen, how you
gonna change anything when it's twenty-five to ten and you're still
sitting on your ass in your underwear? Welfare opens at nine sharp,
same as every other city department." Every investigator cuts corners, if they covered their caseload official, followed the department's
book, they'd work an eighty-hour week and wind up in Bellevue. But
he was saving souls. He knew I had him, but instead of admitting he
was just lazy, he winks at me like we was playing the same game.
"Today's my morning in the field." "Yeah," I says, "plowing."*

92

Which brought Angie's eyebrows up and got me more disgusted, he was such a snot nose! Angie wanted something young she coulda picked a kid from the neighborhood who knew how to keep his mouth shut. I went into the bedroom to catch some sleep, when Angie came in for his clothes she bent down to kiss me but I shoved her off. After he finally got dressed and dragged himself off to work she came back to bed. "Maybe you're right," she says, "I know how you feel but there's something about him that gets to me. He keeps noticing all kinds of things, last night he hadda get up and tiptoe into Nikky's room to see if she sucks her thumb when she's asleep. And he wants to know if she remembers her dreams. I mean, it's weird in a way, but it's different." I didn't feel like saying anything, I rolled over onto my stomach. "I think he's a fake," I mumbled, "I think he's a fake and the kind of guy never knows what he wants, I think you're asking for trouble." She poked me in the ribs with her forefinger, she wasn't being playful. "I'm old enough," she said. "I can handle whatever kinda trouble he makes."

Quickly turning to rain.

So what if he ripped up their requisition slip, he would've
got just as wet with a cane. Or crutches. He limped faster than
some people his age walked, could have shielded his scalp
from the water which soaked his hair and edged down his neck
to dampen his already soggy collar. But he was too stubborn
to wear a hat. And he got splattered because he was trying
to count forward from 1914, not because he couldn't
limp out of range of their hooves. He never even heard those
horses.

Sixteen, prancing in formation, matched pairs, only a fraction
have thoroughbred blood but they look good, they're supposed
to, Department always hires top trainers to do their
purchasing.

NEIGHBORHOOD LEGEND   Some Russian count trains them. Used to command the Cossacks
who guarded the Czar. Hope he's learned something since then.

Urban cavalry for the uptown show routes. Mostly
ceremonial, occasionally dragooned into pesky bureaucratic
duties, it demeans a slick-brushed, shiny-maned horse to carry
a thigh-booted cop writing a parking ticket. Save them for the
ticker-tape parades, the big politicians' escorts, they're too
high-spirited to squander on administration. Let the computers
handle the traffic, half those tickets never get paid anyway.
Lissen, the stable boys wink at each other, *if these
horses could talk they'd run the Department.*

Gelded stallions, sorrel, chestnut, and bay, stable-free
after a damp morning, snorting curls of white vapor which

95

slowly condense in crisp air. Toss mane, jerk and saw
experimentally, quickly finding the limits of firmly held reins
before polished leather boots dig stirrups into their flanks.
Three quick whistles and a casually up-raised arm move the
column off to reassure rather than conquer, a reminder,
for uptown matrons, of commitments to stability their
grandmothers took for granted. Neat manure pads on watered
uptown streets whet the lunch-leaning appetites of impatient
businessmen, while delicate little girls in white leotards and
ballet slippers tiptoe across a polished studio floor to sway at
French windows, noting the troop's graceless carriage.
Grandchildren of flat-milers, steeplechase, call-to-hounds,
point-to-point, great-grandchildren of the desperate Crimean
cavalry chargers and the spirited mounts of the Honor Guard
of the Hohenzollerns, what egalitarian perversions conspired
to force these overbred relics to prance past idling autos,
snorting in nervous disgust at exhaust fumes, doomed
to bear until pastured the trained but pedestrian bulks of sons
of the old sod whose fathers traditionally doffed their caps to
everyone mounted?

And downtown? Downtown-east, where he got splashed?

No percentage in patrolling those streets. Kids roll marbles
in cobblestone gullies, use pea shooters and air rifles to harass
nervous horseflesh. Patrol heading back to the stables, cops
slumped, rolling, in their saddles, none of them yelled at him
to step back. Matto stared, as they pounded past, at the mud
splotching his already filthy pants and jacket.

I lost my best black shooter in the mud. On tiptoe, trying to
balance, we threw penknives and carved the mud into pie slices. Hide

96

and seek in the long summer evenings, they said Cora would hide
in the alley with anybody but she never hid with me. Only
once. She went first, she thought I was Vince. Soft whisper as I
tiptoed through puddles: "Vince, Vince, hurry, they'll find us." She
only let me feel her breasts under her sailor blouse; her nipples
were damp, her upper lip was sweaty when I tried to kiss her.
"You don't even know how to kiss, you ninny!" Vince had a long
thin one, afterwards he swore to her he didn't know we were
watching from Benny's fire escape when she snuck him into her
room, but she never talked to him again. At first she only let him
feel her up and finger her through her panties, but then Benny
said she was getting hot, she squirmed on her bed till her boobs were
hanging over the edge and when he finally took it out she grabbed
for it and got it into her mouth. I knocked over the lamp because
Benny shoved me trying to lean farther out the window, but nobody
heard Benny's father till he pushed the door open. When the fire
escape stuck I was afraid to jump but Benny's father was after us,
only two landings away. I let go. The others knew how to land, but
my knee went out as soon as I hit the sidewalk. The hospital gave
me a brace and said it would heal without an operation. Afterward
when we yelled at her in the street she just stuck her nose in the air.
Once we made her cry, she was walking home from church with
her mother.

97

"Well what the hell am I supposed to do, Sarge, ask him what he did with the camera?" Cinelli waved Matto to his customary seat and swore into the mouthpiece, so Matto eased into the spindly ladder-backed chair Cinelli set out for the boys and stared at the grillwork patterning Cinelli's face. "Now look, Sarge, you got no right saying that about me, not after all the times I stuck my neck out for you. I'm the one who's taking the risk! What happens if one of them figures it's me who's putting the finger on them? I wouldn't stand a chance! Yeah, I can really rely on the kinda protection you guys would give me, I seen what happened to Calio's old man. So lay off me, Sarge, I told you I didn't see no camera. Sarge, you're holding me up! Sarge, lissen, we won't argue, for old times' sake I'll throw twenty-five bucks into the kitty, but don't push me, Sarge, I'm a poor man. That camera ain't worth fifty bucks to its mother! I don't get no guaranteed pension outa this place, Sarge, and I don't get no paid holidays, either. Thirty bucks, Sarge, that's as high as I go, I gotta clear fifty on the camera just to break even, who's gonna give me eighty bucks for it? Thirty bucks, and you can check the sales slip. Okay? Awright. Yeah, I got his address, but you gotta do me a favor. He's gonna use that money to score, he'll be there when you want him. So wait a day, two days, it don't hurt you none. Otherwise I can't stay in business, it's too risky, you show up on his doorstep twenty minutes after he walks outa here and if he don't figure it out, the next guy will. And then I'm finished, I can't afford to cooperate any more. That's not a threat, Sarge, it's a prediction. Yeah, awright, I'll wait for you. With the address. And your thirty bucks, if somebody's stupid enough to give me eighty for the camera. Don't break your neck." Cinelli slams the phone down and shakes his head

99

at Matto, dozing in his tilted chair. "Sometimes it's hard to figure out who squeezes worse."

Some nerve threshold below the surface of Matto's doze warned him he was being addressed. He slid up to waking, nodded agreement into the tail of Cinelli's sentence. Cinelli sniffed at the accumulation of a day's Out-Patient odors on Matto, his jacket honeycombed with patches and moth holes, trap for bad air. His knee, moreover, still leaked pus; when he shifted, his bandage reminded him, constriction like a damp sponge. The camphor smell Matto catches in his nostrils is actually menthol, constituent of the thick cream Cinelli massages into his scalp to keep his head skin gleaming and flexible. Otherwise flaky patches of dead skin drift down to coat his merchandise.

"I think I'm gonna close up and go home, Dutch. It's shitty outside and nobody's gonna miss me. Let that fat cop sweat a little when he sees my grating locked."

Matto nods, swallows, rubs at an itch in his shoulder and pushes himself up before he remembers to prop. His knee locks, a tumbling half-pivot and hopping, he reaches Cinelli's window ledge to brace, panting at the pain. "Goddam knee," he mumbles at Cinelli. "Hospital fixed me. Needle. Bastards."

Cinelli considered getting him to a doctor, that knee didn't look too good. But another half-hour would bring him dangerously close to rush-hour traffic. He watched Matto catch his breath, clamping his lower lip in a stubborn grimace against the pain, but Matto's bandage was hidden by the bulges of his baggy trousers. Cinelli couldn't guess how ugly the knee would look in its nest of pus, and didn't he always limp? *You feel all your scars in the rain.* And it wasn't pity. *Who'll miss one cane? I'll never get rid of all this junk.* Cinelli's sour hatred for the accumulation which kept him in bondage never interfered with his meticulous storage. He chose one of twenty similar curved yellow woods, rubber-tipped, and carried it out to Matto.

"Here. It's slippery out there. You'll get along better with this."

Matto nodded at Cinelli and then at the cane cradled in his right hand, let himself lean on it, testing, before he limped into the wet street. Cinelli switched off his lights, set the alarm buzzer, and decided, while locking the grate, against entering the gift of the cane in his voluminous ledger. *When they auction off all this junk, it won't even cover a year's rent on my plot. Who'll miss one cane?*

Three-legged now, limping through intermittent drizzle, chatter surrounds him. He edges through swaying schoolgirl shoulders. Stiffening against their raucous voices he shuts his nose to their smell, his clenched right hand on his cane forces passage through the crowd's center. Usually he was shy of contact, but today he barged through, knocking raincoats, slippery cord jackets, once a fragment of jutting tit, did he aim high? "Watch it, old man!" But he wouldn't waste words, burst through the crowd's rim before he realized they were all grouped around Furco, cowering against the shoemaker's window. His lower jaw limp, hands scrabbling in his pockets, shoulders so slumped his suede jacket collar rode high over his D.A. Two of them his challengers, the shorter one very light-skinned but neither as tall as Furco. On the fringe of the crowd, tense white faces, he recognized Furco's friends. Why the hell didn't they help him out?

NEIGHBORHOOD
LEGEND

Whenever you need a couple of yards you give the ball to Furco.

He led our gang as long as I can remember. And he called all the shots, when those Spics from the Strip came over he busted at least three arms.

It's not just his looks, he's got a reputation to maintain. Any girl he takes out knows she's got a white name in the neighborhood.

We could never persuade him to sing in the choir. But he's always conducted himself like a gentleman.

"Call two against one fair?" Matto mumbled, itching to swing his cane against black heads. Furco's eyes were shifting constantly to avoid the stares of the sullen crowd. Too quiet. "You should've kept your mouth shut," one of the two

103

crowding Furco said. "Nobody was pressuring you, you could've kept your mouth shut." Furco shook his head. "I didn't say anything." Somebody snickered. Shuffling feet scraping damp pavement, rustle of rainclothes, they edged forward, squeezing him, what the hell was he doing there, a workingman with a bum knee? "Gimme some room," Matto mumbled, lost his balance, staggered, took refuge in the milliner's doorway. Rows of narrowed eyes in set faces, scowling, examined him briefly before turning back to Furco. Who was sweating now, pinned against the window, the smaller one shaking his head as he slapped his fist into his palm.

"They should cut your tongue outa your mouth, Furco! Hurley's gonna get at least two years on account of you."

A girl's voice, scorn for Furco, another useless target, meanwhile Hurley was out of circulation, Hurley wasn't her man but another one sent up, locked away, come back two years later looking ten years older and for what? The same load of crap! And all we got is another white boy crawling in the gutter, swearing his hands are clean. "Look, you got me wrong! I didn't do it. Hurley was my friend too, I didn't want him to get sent up. I didn't do it. I never said a word about it. I swear before God and the Holy Mother, I didn't say anything. May God strike me dead if I'm lying—I didn't do it!"

Matto watched his suede jacket soak up puddle water as he groveled. "Sounds like a sick dog." Girl clicked her tongue against the roof of her mouth and Matto realized that Furco had saved himself.

"Get up, goddam you! Get up, you yellow bastard!"

104

They couldn't stoke their anger. Trying to glare at him, begging, on his knees. Shrugged their shoulders. Furco's arms shielded his face, quivered from kicks he expected momentarily, too stricken to realize his fear had pulled him through. "I didn't say anything, I didn't, you gotta believe me, guys, I swear to God I never said anything!" The same girl released them into embarrassed clumps, turning their backs and shaking their heads as they edged away from the shoemaker's window. "Let him crawl. No point stomping worms."

And Matto considered reaching a hand down to Furco still on his knees, a steadying hand to hoist him up and wipe off the mud that coated him. Instead he knocked a smashed cardboard milk carton over the crumbling lip of curb into the gutter with the rubber tip of Cinelli's cane before limping across the street.

Even their blood stinks. Louie's brother couldn't get the smell off his jacket, I threw my pants away. As soon as we turned into his block all their radios started playing, they were waiting for us. But it didn't do him no good, we hadda go over the roofs but we caught him, Louie's gun in his neck while we broke his arms. Jesus rot your soul in hell, he kept screaming, until we bashed in his nose and his blood choked him. He was supposed to be tough. Slipping some tramp our money for her kids. Probably his kids. Next time you wanna play Santa Claus, use your own money, Louie said, he never took off his gloves. I shoulda worn old pants, I couldn't stand the smell.

"Get outa my way!" Matto mumbles, brushing a slight Chinese boy and then recoiling off a covey of Negro girls;

105

surly, they ignored him, tossing kerchiefed heads as he shifted behind them. "Goddammit, you let me through!"

"Take it easy, mister, who you pushing?" Nostrils flaring she turns on him, high cheekbones, high arching breasts. "Push you right on your fucking black ass," he mumbles, lower than she can hear, a twitch in his forearm almost sends his hand jamming into her tits, but as the other girls bunch behind her, he slides past her shoulder into the street, a truck squeals to a stop but the driver, seeing his cane, checks his curses. "Ah, forget it, Dolores, the guy's crippled."

"Oh yeah? Well he still got no right to push me like that!"

When the Durwent, *off Curaçao, the number three tank—what kind of a girl was she? Why did they pick me, I wasn't the only one had the keys. The milk I brought she used for her baby, I saw her. Holding her breasts with her fingers for me. "No, not beautiful, bad, like snakes, dry, no milk for my baby." Nigger baby, so black against her, crying until she opened one of the cans I brought, a whole crateful, and got my milk into a bottle. Then he came in. I didn't understand. Even after he said he knew I carried a key to the stockroom, I didn't believe it. She could do that? His baby? She called me Angel, when she had me inside her she made such sounds, I felt like a king! She could do that? None of the others could make such sounds. But they did it, the two of them, they made the trap for me. He knew what taverns I always went to, and once I saw her what could I do? Any man would fall for her. For her. They did it for her. For her baby. His baby. Their baby. They told me not to fight him but I knew I had to kill him. They told me he was good with a knife but I thought the Lord would help me kill him, after what they did to me. But they said he could've killed me, after the second cut I couldn't see, on my knees with fire burning my ribs, they said he spit on his knife and threw it overboard. They kicked him off the ship but she was back there waiting for him.*

"My daughter-in-law called up the other day, she says my grandson don't wanna go to school any more, just sits home and plays his drums all day long. You ever hear anything so crazy?" And as Matto shook his head, toying with his last few swallows of the coffee they always served him for free, at least one cup (privileges of the club, they told him, after all, you're practically a charter member). "You sure you don't wanna try a game or two?" Nobody remembered he didn't play dominoes. He shook his head, watching Caruso's stubby fingers fondle the white-dotted rectangles, arranging patterns to outwit himself, nobody to accommodate him. "I can't play. Never learned how."

Once the Vitello Social and Athletic Club had fielded a touch-football team, complete with substitutes, and played a basketball league every Wednesday evening where uniforms were compulsory. As well as dances most Saturday nights of the season, and a semi-formal in St. Aloysius's Hall every three months. Matto had once been nominated for assistant sergeant-at-arms; his pulse raced during the balloting, dreaming of standing, sentinel-stiff at the door, decorated with the crimson and white ribbon of office. But Parisi's brother-in-law won, they didn't announce the tallies because they were embarrassed nobody else voted for Matto. Now only the domino players remained, two years ago someone had finally removed the faded Roosevelt photo-portrait in its tarnished gilt frame, only Kennedy stared from the peeling walls, black borders wreathing his square-jawed intensity. Matto, glancing now at the small dead eyes below the boyish lock of hair, wondered, as always, whether it was somebody's son killed in the war.

"You hear what they're trying to pull now?" Caruso shook

his head. "Wanna take over a school uptown. Run it themselves. So they can teach all the little monkeys breaking and
entering. I met Louisa in Rocky's the other day, she says she's
trying to pull some strings to get into the new projects near
First Avenue, the Counselor promised to help. Everybody's
fed up in her building, they got storm windows and police
locks and iron bars on all the windows and still five people
were broken into, last month alone. And they don't just take
what they want any more, either. They tear up the whole
apartment. For spite."

Matto nodded, yawning. The squat Puerto Rican woman
hired out of the club's diminishing treasury clumped past
on floppy felt slippers, lugging her bucket and rags to the front
window. Matto smelled the thin ammonia mixture as
some of the bluish liquid sloshed over the bucket's side and
trickled along the floorboards; when Caruso turned back to his
table to nurse his dominoes, Matto closed his eyes. His Aunt
Carrie used ammonia to scrub her windows without a
rope looping her thick waist securely to Geracimo's iron bed-
stead and her kitchen table. Clean white kerchief, once
her grandmother's dishtowel, knotted at the base of her thick
bun of gray hair, lower window wedged firmly down on
her thick knees, she straddled the narrow ledge and wiped,
methodically. "I don't look down and I don't think about
it," she explained to Matto, bunching the flesh of the
back of his neck to squeeze, like a kitten's. "Anybody could
keep their balance, it's all in the head."

After she gave the front window a final disinterested swipe,
the Puerto Rican cleaning woman lit the lone neon display

bulb before she switched on the club's interior lights. Matto
blinked in the sudden yellow haze while Caruso stared glumly
at the light above their table, tatters of festive shade scorched
as the bulb swung feebly on the end of its cord. "Never have
any dances any more, like we used to in the old days. Dutch,
you used to dance, you came here all the time with a good-
looking young one on your arm, you used to tear up the dance
floor." Matto lets Caruso thump his shoulder, watches Caruso's
phlegm coat the table top as he wheezes noiseless laughter
and nods agreement, although he never learned to dance, the
one girl he brought to the club was too shy to teach him.
If she knew. They sat at the most secluded table, shaded in
half-light, far from the crowded dance floor, each time he
glanced at her she smiled, tremulously. Nobody had ever
taken her to the club before, almost no one had ever asked her
out, let alone brought candy for her mother and flowers for
her wrapped proudly in a green swirl of crinkly paper. The
night crew quit teasing him, Matto ready to tie the knot and
why not, he was certainly taking home enough and the girl
was innocent, docile, pathetically eager to please. "You do
whatever he wants," her mother warned her. "Even if he talks
about you to the whole neighborhood, it's better than being
an old maid. Besides he's the kind that keeps his mouth shut."
Her mother also guessed he was incapable of taking advantage
so they ceded him the front parlor, took to bed after dinner
every Saturday night prepared to shut their ears to whatever
squeaking menaced the worn springs of the horsehair sofa.
Matto barely touched her. Money constantly in pocket, he
bought himself his first new suit and a pair of blue suede shoes,
pointy toes but no alligator trim, he'd consulted with Jeff

who'd advised against flashiness. Savored his stomach's jitters
as he dressed for their Saturday night ritual, fifteen minutes
to knot the fat V of his tie and anchor it securely beneath his
bobbing Adam's apple with the trim point of a gold collar pin,
enjoying the luxurious slip of the white-on-white shirt against
his scarred forearms. Hair cream and after-shave lotion and
approval from the boys at Tony's, a quick beer before picking
her up, he'd sworn off hard liquor and smelled like a youngish
man with prospects who'd sampled the world before deciding
to settle down. Nobody deciphered her name from his
mumbled introductions, but they all decided she adored him,
her timidity passed for affection. When he bent to kiss her
she closed her eyes and submitted; though his hands could
gentle quivering small animals he could never stop the shivers
which furrowed her back till he released her, granting the
warmth of his companionable arm wherein she snuggled,
relieved. She was afraid to fail him, nobody had ever taught
her how to kiss and he had known so many girls, would he
laugh if she confessed? She held her tongue but prayed she
wouldn't lose him, baked him cookies and brought him
sandwiches for his long night's work which he accepted
without trying to describe the feasts Al cooked for them. Once
he started to tell her just how different she was from the other
women he'd known but he stammered, stared at his carefully
brushed suede shoes and finally suggested they go uptown,
she'd never been to Radio City. (Afterwards she told her
mother he had almost proposed.) Once at the circus she clapped
her hands and squealed with delight as the spotlights circled
the bareback team, girls in sequined tights, twinkling bells on
prancing white horses. Pressure mounted on him, mother

constantly extolling the girl's domestic accomplishments, with more experience Matto would've recognized the father's beleaguered countenance as warning that he was being prodded to deliver the *coup de grace.* "When's the wedding bells, Dutch?" the crew always asked, usually he blushed. Nights he worked he considered whether he wanted a woman to live through years with, someone you didn't have to pay for it, maybe he could show her how. Iron his shirts and dust her mother's furniture which had already, tactfully, been offered; fry his eggs every morning and confess, tearfully, that she'd lost one of his new green socks in the wash. A hint of mustache spoiled her lip line but her mother brushed a hundred strokes into her hair every evening, Matto day-dreamed of nuzzling through that thickness to lick the taut skin of her back and gently ease her over as her tentative hands wandered through his hair and finally passionate, guided him. But he never told her. Or touched her. And after the Polack squealed he was too ashamed to explain. Her mother guessed a man like him would never leave the neighborhood, the girl could've found him and explained that it didn't matter. He would've kissed her tiny feet and married her as fast as St. Aloysius's could've arranged it. Maybe. But her mother decided he was no longer suitable, an old maid was preferable to a criminal's wife, whatever tiny will had flared into feeble life under Matto's gentle hands was extinguished. She let them consign him. And her. They all forgot Matto's girl, he always mumbled her name and her face was too plain. Matto avoided the block she lived on and the tiny park where she sat with the neighborhood mothers, plagued by a nagging conviction that he was her last chance.

113

Heavy scrape of his chair as Caruso pushed himself up after jumbling all the dominoes into their worn cheesebox holder. "I'm going, Dutch. Gotta feed the dog and catch up on the paper. Take it easy."

Matto nodded, wondering where he fed to keep that stomach. No one else would come in till after dinner. He dozed for another half-hour, shook himself awake, pushed out of his chair and limped across the street toward Tony's.

Shoved at cold hands kneading his side, then squirmed across cushions, his toenails catching and scratching snags of worn brocade. Burrowing into an unfamiliar pillow Laurie must've shoved over onto his side, he remembered some objection to the dishes which meant they were still stacked into the sink, to be washed before shaving in the morning. Or no hot water. "Fuck it," he mumbled and rolled over again.

"Hey, c'mon, move over! Let me in. You were hot enough to get me into bed a couple of hours ago!" Slippery muslin or gauze over warm flesh but cold hands prodded him, rolled him over, pinned against fabric, what the hell happened to the bed? What're you doing home so early, he thought to ask, though Laurie never wore nightgowns and there was a taste of something gummy in his mouth that he could sniff on whoever was squirming next to him. "I can't make my tongue work, how the hell did my mouth get so gummed up? What time is it?"

She giggled and he heard Nikky's laugh caught in her throatiness. "Must be four. At least. I hadda wait to make sure Sal was asleep. Takes him almost an hour sometimes to work up his big bubbly snore but once he starts hitting those long Z's you could bite his ear off and he wouldn't wake up." So only a thickness of wall away, in Angie's musty bedroom, Sal was wrapped in flowered sheets next to a tangle of bedclothes. Maybe his arm nuzzled a pillow for companionship? The kid shivered. "You really take some chances. You're lucky Sal don't drink that sweet stuff, he gets a hell of a lot meaner than you when he's really pissed." Warm breath into the folds of his neck, almost absently she licked at his ear but already her hands were busy. "That's why I told you to buy it. You always

115

said you liked Marsala and I figured he wouldn't touch it."
Sal had actually dozed off halfway through her story, when
she finished she kicked him awake. "Before we hit the sack
I think I would like a little nightcap, for a celebration of the
swell time both of you sports have shown me. I think if one
of you gets up off his ass you could make Nino's before he
closes, I'll even lay out the money. Make sure it's something
sweet," she shouted, the kid was already bouncing down the
steps, humming; if whatever she had in mind needed stimulus
then he was pleased to supply it. They started by drinking it
on the rocks, both of them grinning at Sal's grumpy refusal.
"Look at him already taking his shoes and socks off, that's
really getting domestic." Sal, head lolling, stretched the weight
of his bunched shoulder muscles and glanced sheepishly down
at his shoes; the kid watched his face ease into weariness and,
ashamed, decided to lay off. But Angie had a scene she was
trying to provoke. "Why don't you curl up on the couch and
watch some television? Nikky's not ready for bed yet." They
drank too quickly after Sal padded across to flop on her couch,
began a chase in which they mashed Sal's feet and tumbled
across him as they weaved through furniture. Angie tried to
lead him in a parody of a tango ended by his stumble over
Nikky's medicine chest. He wrestled Angie down as he
sprawled, bedroom curtains blocking Sal's view from the couch
as Nikky howled for her toys. "Can't you get rid of him somehow? Just for tonight?" Handful of ample tit but his other
hand, fumbling for her crotch, deflected; warm furry tongue
in his ear for reward. "Behave yourself." Whispered. And then
shouted: "Jesus Christ, you goddam clumsy bastard, you almost
ripped my housecoat! Nikky shut up, for Chrissake, your

116

doctor's cabinet's made of iron, he couldn't break it if he ran over it with a garbage truck!"

"It's not iron it's only made of tin! And he's already made a great big dent in it!" Sobbing, she consented to be gathered to Angelina's breast to be rocked, comforted, then scolded gently into sleep, while the kid lurched into the living room to collapse into an armchair. Sal bulked a dull menace from the couch, somebody had shut the sound off but the tube still flickered, a much bluer light than usual but the kid couldn't focus the image. "Such an interesting picture. What did people use to get themselves to sleep before the late-night movies?"

"Why don't you go home? You're a pain in the ass sober and a pain in the ass drunk. It looks like you can't even hold your wine, let alone your liquor. Nikky's asleep and Angie wants some sleep. Why don't you go upstairs where you belong?"

"You wanna go to bed you go to bed, but don't you decide when I'm ready for bed," Angie shouted at Sal. "I make up my own mind in this apartment, who the hell are you to throw your weight around? You don't own me and you never will!"

"Now what the hell's eating you? I didn't put in a sixteen-hour shift just to take his lip! I'm tired! I think he's a pain in the ass, I need to ask your permission before I kick him out?"

"You got the right to use your gun, off duty as well as on, as long as you show your badge first or in some way identify yourself. If the suspect is fleeing, order him to halt in a commanding voice and identify yourself as an officer of the law.

117

If he insists on his flight, you may fire a warning shot into the air. This will deter all but the hardened criminal, whose head can safely be blown off. You could charge me with interfering with a police officer in the pursuit of his pleasure. Molesting the Department's women. I'll tell the court I saw the label imprinted on Angie's neck, property of the New York City Police Department, but I thought it was a joke, just like your tattoo." Mother looped across a fat red heart, impulse at eighteen, he'd confided to Angie, seduced by swaying raffia in a tattooer's window, grimy woman shawled in a red kerchief beckoned, but instead of gypsy ass the quick prick of the tattooer's needle, five dollars lighter but bearing an emblem later repudiated by long-sleeved shirts, even in summertime, occasionally even in bed.

"You shut up." Angie swore at him, worried about another small betrayal, will Sal assume everyone talks in bed? "You take everything too seriously. You can't stop scoring points. And you," over her shoulder to Sal, "this ain't a rest home, you can't take me for granted. You get your own way so much you got spoiled, giving orders comes easy to you. You wanna go to bed you know where it is, if not, there's a load of dishes in the sink could stand some washing, especially if you're looking forward to breakfast in the morning. And as for you," she turned back to the kid, "stop holding yourself up by my drapes, you'll rip them off their runners. Take a blanket and go lie down on the couch and sleep it off, you'll only stink up your own apartment. Maybe we'll all feel better in the morning."

"But you had other plans all along," he whispered as she snuggled against him after wriggling her nightgown off, she was already moist, her soft hair matted. "He was so pissed off he could hardly talk," she whispered into his ear, shivers down his half-drugged nerves toward the small of his back as she worked him, fingers nibbling his nipples, his ribs, down the slope of his stomach to his thighs. Somewhere a reflex reminded him she liked him passive, small choice at this hour. "I never seen him like that before, I got into bed and he stood by the side of the bed, then he pretended to stare out the window. I let him wait, I could almost hear him trying to figure out what to say. Finally I gave up waiting for him to decide. 'You're not a horse,' I said to him, 'you never learned to sleep on your feet, for Chrissake get into bed and stop brooding. I'm just disgusted with both of you, that's all.' When he finally climbed in he turned his face to the wall like he didn't intend to have anything to do with me. I changed his mind fast enough."

Triumphant, she giggled. The best of both worlds, he thought, took his time. She stayed on the couch with him till dawn for reward, finally kissed his forehead and rearranged his blanket, tucking him in, ridges of frayed cushion creasing his stomach, before tiptoeing back to Sal's snores. What penance, he thought, and yawned, careful not to cramp his neck muscles till they locked. This can't last. Somebody'll slip up, Laurie, I hope I can manage to pick up the pieces. "Who's Nikky?" Maybe she even prodded my ribs with a precise forefinger, I woke up like a shot, tremors in my neck sounding alarms, I faked grogginess. "Huh?" Do even my dreams turn traitor? "You were mumbling something about Nikky when I came in." Squinting at the light she finally switches on, little-girl dress I hate slips over her shoulders, always relieved to see her

119

flat stomach appear beneath it, they ever ask you at work how many months? "Nikky? Nikky who?" "I don't know Nikky who, that's why I asked. You were mumbling Nikky, like a curse, just as I started to switch the light on, you were so clear I thought you were talking to me and then I listened but it was just Nikky Nikky Nikky. You were very angry at her." Angelina talking through my dreams, scolding? But I saw my way out. "Jealous?" She grinned, carefully shrugging her spiky shoulders. "Should I be?" Touché for you, my love, you found the right counter and turned away to lay out your morning clothes, another of my suggestions you fought till I was forced to convince you it was eminently sensible. Drifting toward his threshold he watched her scrabble awake, blinded chick, soap tearing her eyes, botched makeup, at least lay your clothes out the night before so the subway people don't discover you're wearing my socks! Only Harrison's filter-paper coffee finally woke her. He reminded himself to stay awake, attentive, stifle his weariness enough to grant her due with his flesh in order to settle any hovering suspicions; luckily, he thought, why bother to stifle the ripple of pride which swelled him momentarily, I can always manage. Dawn was staining Angie's curtains. He yawned. She pecked me so softly before she padded in to Sal maybe she'll fix me breakfast before I climb upstairs. No hope of burrowing into her bed, he'll probably sleep till noon. What haunts Laurie? She still lets me get away with every little game I play. I wait for her to sink her nails into my shoulders, turn me around to face her anguished stare. "Just what do you think you're trying to do to me?" Dozing now, he barely registered first bird cries. "Hey. Wake up. C'mon, wake up!"

120

Dirty light under his eyelids. "Go away. Go away and let me sleep. My head hurts."

"C'mon, c'mon wake up." Shaking him roughly, nails into his shoulders. "It's still early, hurry up, let's get back into bed. Sal's gone. I guess I woke him up climbing back in, or maybe he never really went to sleep, maybe he faked all that snoring to find out what we were up to. I yawned and pretended I was dead tired but I could feel him rigid beside me, he must've laid there forever without moving, I couldn't think of a thing to say. Finally he got up and put his clothes on and didn't even look at me, he tiptoed out so he wouldn't wake Nikky. He didn't even slam the door."

Later, joints screaming after another bout he swore he couldn't complete and completed anyway, through her ministrations and an edge of something close to panic which made her desperate, he locked his fingers under the crown of his head and watched her body barely stirring in sleep. Only an hour or two till Nikky wakes up, and Angie already thinking she'd made a mistake to let Sal go. Nothing to look forward to, he considered gathering up his clothes and heading upstairs, at least he'd be guaranteed uninterrupted sleep. Couldn't have two men walking out on her in one night. He yawned and turned away, Carson was right to chew my ass out. My work is falling apart, I can't even keep my Residuals filed. And while she was at it, she thought she might as well mention my hours. Erratic. Wouldn't dispute that, Carson. So I mumbled about strain, home pressures, hardly getting any sleep at night, keeping my eyes on the scuffed tips of my working shoes, don't enjoy airing my dirty linen. You never used to mumble, she snapped at me, now you sneak around this place like you got acne, what's happening to you? Carson, I'll send you a memo. Just the usual kinds of troubles. She sniffed, not convinced. Usual troubles don't affect you like they do most people, I suppose. You're really coming apart at the seams. Listen, you want a couple of days' sick leave? Get broiled on some beach, give your head a rest? I could even cover for you at home if it's necessary, you figure out how to explain your tan when you get back. I'd thought about it before. Nah, it's not worth it, Carson, I'd peel for a week after, puffed up like some lobster, and instead of trying to think my way out of this I'd probably spend all my time trying to bed somebody I'd hate as soon as I'd had her. I don't know how to get out of this. And then, carefully: Maybe you could figure out where I could get some free therapy? It might help. She nodded, measuring me. Sure. I could probably chisel my therapist to give you a reduction. Like ten bucks an hour. That's half what I pay, you'd have to guarantee to be twice as interesting.

No problem, he'd said immediately, and then, realizing the judgment, tried to backtrack. I mean, the content's a lot more sordid. She only laughed at him, he could never guess what would cause offense. You take care of yourself. She waved a finger at him as he nodded out her office door. I mean it, I worry about you. She does mean it, he thought, still not ready to sleep, I wonder what she sees. What do I look like to Carson? Would it help me to know? And woke with a jolt, tumbling off some bridge again, stomach grounding him. It can't last. Even if Sal keeps his mouth shut, half the neighborhood must be wise, Angie's got girlfriends she spends hours with in the beauty parlor. And Nikky? Does Nikky babble to her playmates about the men she discovers sharing her mother's bed? Why do I bother to propitiate her, I can't stand the way she minces. Angie's made her into a little bitch and then she turns on me when I play up to her. Cute? You give me a pain in the ass. Whatta you know about it, you look at her ass in that little red sunsuit and all you can think of is whether she'll have hot pants for you by the time she's thirteen. You tease her like she already knows what she's got, and how to use it! Just don't think you're so special because she plays up to you now, a month after you move outa the neighborhood she won't even remember your name. A threat or a promise? Probably neither. Moreover she was accurate, something about the wiggle of Nikky's buttocks when she squirmed over me aroused me to visions of tasting her tiny but damp slit and then corkscrewing my tongue up her dainty anus. But other times I was convinced it was her need for me or somebody whose shoes I barely filled to which I responded; what about those nights when, too prickly to sleep, I watched by Nikky's cot to catch her dreams before they tumbled her up and woke her, sobbing for Angie? Having despaired of Laurie's complications, was I choosing a hand-me-down, a bastard through whom to play out my fantasies of fatherhood? Whatever I was doing, she always responded, cradled her head on my shoulder and nuzzled her damp cheeks against my neck, even murmured my name as I eased her into bed without waking Angelina. How many nights did Nikky lie in my arms and let me stroke her till her sobbing ceased, before her head burrowed into the warm hollows of Angelina's body? If, in her rootings, her tiny ass occasionally grazed my swelling, can I really be blamed? Men commit unthinkable acts with far less provocation, but night

123

after night I played the gray foster father, anonymous comforter, I did my duty without caring whether Nikky realized
whose neck she nuzzled on her easy passage to motherflesh.

How many nights did Sal get seduced by sudden intimations of
parentage? Maybe Nikky's sobbing never woke him, chainsaw
sleeper, Angelina awake and squirming out of her stripy sheets
to pad across her linoleum, scoop Nikky up and bundle her into
bed before he ever fought clear of the weariness blanketing
him. In the morning he found himself part of a trio, how the
hell did Nikky wind up in bed with us? Did Angie play her
cat's games with Sal, or was it only in me she sensed how much
the child excited? Cuddling Nikky till she relaxed, alert till the
slow breath against the pillow signaled her safely dreaming,
Angelina's small but cunning hand crept down to me and
stroked, teased, cupped and molded till I was taut and throbbing, locked against the innocent restraint of Nikky's midget
rump and thighs. I never reached out to touch her face but I
could sense her grin as she savored my helplessness—did Sal
also honor Nikky's sleep? Some nights she worked so zealously
to rouse me she also stirred herself; then she'd ease over Nikky
to yield me a back entrance. But the sigh as I finally slipped myself in was shared, for when my hands, bored with the soft
ridges of her shoulder muscles or the birthmarks dotting her
back, reached round to cup and fondle her breasts, they found
either a tell-tale wet on distended nipples or Nikky's head still
fastened, her lips sucking in time to my strokes. Often two pairs
of hands traced Nikky's frail shoulders or caressed the soft
tangles of her curls, our fingers joined in her hair and then sep-
arated to explore the miniature hollows of her neck and armpits, the tiny bumps of her spine. What legacy, for Nikky, some

shrink may someday reveal, but what harvest for me, never gathered with Laurie?

Waiting for Nikky's awakening whimper he finally fell asleep. Below him in the streets another Matto limps home, undetected—

SAL *Fifty men was on duty downtown-east that night, same's any other. On the streets, slapping their hands together, cruising in squad cars, not to mention the all-night guys at the precincts or staffing Control at Headquarters. Fifty guys out on the street, any hour of the morning, whatta they see? Evil incarnate? Nah, mostly drunks. Call 'em in, mark 'em on the chart, seven o'clock milkman's run will sweep them all in, a shower and a meal. Department's catering service, sleep it off, Mac, get sobered up for thirty days in the workhouse. Somebody calls in a silhouette in a warehouse window. But it turns out to be the night watchman. Fight in a basement, bring them both in, scared shitless. Maybe three, maybe four murders a night. And a thousand guys exactly like him walking the streets, suppose we stop each one and shake him down, whatta we learn? We ain't mind-readers and we don't play our hunches. We let him go. We let almost everybody go.*

and the kid tiptoes into the bathroom, dried sperm flaking off as he guides his piss. Don't flush the toilet! Water pipes rise through three more apartments to the roof, a latticework of pipes and joints honeycombing the building: Serafina kneeling by her bed fumbling over her beads, Rosie knitting under an unshaded lampbulb, Angelo shivering in his top bunk with his blankets tangled in the railings. The kid tapped himself dry thinking Matto's building was noisier, steam clanged through

125

his busted pipes, and his knee might've throbbed so bad he couldn't sleep nights.

ANGELINA   *Plenty of people can't sleep nights, he don't deserve special considera-tion. He was a loser, buster, don't waste your pity.* I seen him plenty of times down at Tony's, in her black belted raincoat she always turned heads when she pushed through the door, chorus of, "Angie, baby!" but only a cool nod for answer. "The girl's got guts, you gotta hand it to her." "I'd like to hand it to her, right on the counter, sling her ass up, prop her back against those hogsheads, wrap those legs around me and whale it into her." "Uh-uh, buddy, that's only for New York's finest, you gotta be wearing a badge." Knowing what they saw and sniggered after, but satisfied as long as they granted her quick passage to the bar, no fat hands snaking out to graze a tit or fondle a buttock, she sips her gin-and-tonic, Sal's influence, used to chug down straight Scotch until he told her the least she could do was to drink like a lady. *I seen him plenty of times down at Tony's, he always sat by himself at the curve of the bar closest to the door, and he always huddled into himself like a turtle, his elbows cradling his head. We called him Dutch because he'd fight like hell before he'd let you buy him anything, one beer was his limit. I tried to make him memorize the roads down to Baltimore once, he was thinking of hitch-hiking but he couldn't remember the route numbers. I only found out the following Christmas he actually made it down there. Say more than hello and he'd blush, you could paralyze him by touching his shoulder, he couldn't look a woman in the face with-out stammering.*

LAURIE   *(Staring out the window as the train plods south from Harrison's place outside New Rochelle, water tanks and frame houses slipping*

126

past) From what the papers said he seemed like such a dismal sort of man.

ANGELINA *He was always skinny, always. You know what he eats? C'mere, I'll show you. (In front of Joe's, her raincoat collar hoisted to keep the raw wind off her neck, she beckons through the grimy, steam-coated window.) Coffee. That's what he lives on. Coffee and a roll for breakfast, coffee and a ham sandwich for lunch, soup and coffee for dinner. He'll nurse that coffee for hours, does he ever talk to you?*

JOE *I wouldn't exactly call it talk. We do a routine that's a little better than grunting at each other, I would say occasionally words get ex-changed. But he ain't messy, though, he's a careful eater, never spills nothing, hands me his dishes over the counter and wipes up his place which I always tell him not to bother with, I think he feels bad he can't leave me no tip. The times when he ain't working he avoids my place, I have to catch him on the street and force him inside to eat a meal on the cuff. One winter he ate off me for three weeks while he wasn't working and soon's he's back to work he brings me this sheet of notebook paper, the rings torn like some kid ripped it out of his notebook, with all the meals he ate every day for three weeks written down with the prices besides them. "The only thing I didn't know," he says, "one Friday morning you made me French toast, it's not listed on the menu."*

LAURIE *I thought he couldn't read.*

SAL *The boys always took care of him, he should've known he'd never starve. As soon as he banged up his knee they put him on the Express crew at the warehouse.*

127

CARBONE   *Not because we felt sorry for him. He tried harder to keep his mind on what he was doing he woulda saved himself a lotta misery. (Peak tilted on his red hunting cap, flannel shirt soaked with sweat as he slaps a gloved hand on the worn ridge of the concrete loading platform.) We were just protecting ourselves. Wherever he thought that goddam liquor came from, he saw damn well it didn't have no state or federal tax stamps on it. He keeps wandering around the neighborhood with that bum knee and he gets hungry, anybody who wants some cheap information can buy him right off the sidewalk. Even the fuzz. Especially the fuzz. Not that he'd open his mouth so easy, especially for the kind of dough the fuzz shell out, but if he ain't working he's gotta buy his eats somehow.*

SAL   *(Out of uniform in a housing project playground) We never shell out a penny more than we have to, you'd be surprised how much information we get for nothing. Most people like to talk, especially to us, and we got our ways of encouraging the ones who don't. We run a heavier payroll than in the old days, but that's because there's so many new types to keep tabs on. (Prods a little man in a zipped-up windbreaker.) What do you know about Matto?*

MAN   *(Shrugging) Who watches a guy like him?*

LAURIE   *(On her roof, shaking damp sheets into a stiff wind before pinning them to sagging lines where they billow and flap) You always think we don't appreciate you, but when it comes down to it, you don't know very much.*

SAL   *Lady, whatta you know about anything? We're holding the city together!*

128

LAURIE   *Not for me!*

ANGELINA   *Bullshit! How come you always take cabs after midnight?*

SAL   *Lissen, you seen his picture maybe three times in the papers, right? You wanna tell me which one of these three guys is him? (Three men, two holding hats in their hands, stare dumbly out through a circle of lights. They try not to blink.) Stand up straight there, Number Two! Well? You wanna see profile?*

LAURIE   *(Over the phone, nervously) This is so silly, they plaster the number all over New York and the one time I have to dial it, I can't remember. Oh look, officer, I'm sorry to bother you, but there's a man been hanging around outside for hours now, I know it's silly but I'm a little afraid to go home by myself, I thought he looked a little— there, that one there.*

SAL   *Two steps forward, Number One.*

LOUDSPEAKER   *Joe Volpe, thirty-seven, no fixed address. Charged and convicted, petty larceny, 1957. Charged and convicted, breaking and entering, 1962. Charged, armed robbery, insufficient evidence, 1964. Charged, assault and battery, charges dropped, 1964. Charged, assault with a deadly weapon, case pending, 1965.*

ANGELINA   *(Staring in disgust at the kid nuzzling into her pillow) Another little man!*

LAURIE   *I'm sorry to be making so much trouble for you, but it's much more difficult than you might think. In the dark they all look so much alike.*

Emilie Citti, forty-seven. Men's Shelter, sometimes Salvation Army Home. Seventeen convictions, drunk and disorderly. Eight convictions, loitering. Five convictions, vagrancy.

SAL *(Uptown beat, tight-lipped, blacks on the corner swivel to face him as he approaches, stop their talk as he swaggers past, apparently unconcerned but he hears their curses) Amateur's job. If we wanted a positive identification from you we'd get it, stack him so you'd pick him out in a minute. But it's hard, ain't it; you'd be surprised how many pros never recognize their old man under these lights. We got our ways. Eventually we'll have something on everybody, the city'll move or stop because we tell it to. You worry a lot in cabs? (Laurie gropes her way out of the deserted skeleton of Penn Station, past the wrecking crew's scaffolding, her heels skidding over the temporary planking covering the sidewalk. She whirls her white plastic rainhat at an off-duty cab streaking south for Brooklyn. His brakes squeal. "I'm going downtown. Downtown!" she screeches. He looks her over while she stammers her address.)*

ANGELINA *Big surly buck. Not bad looking, as they come.*

SAL *(The cab cruises downtown through empty streets, a bad connection in a street lamp flickers eerie noon.) Well, if you can't find a white hack driver, your first job's the licence. Memorize the name and number under the picture, though with most of the niggers driving nights the picture ain't there or if it is, it's the wrong one. But you don't even know enough to do that, so just sit there biting your nails, hoping he doesn't realize how nervous you are. What are you gonna be able to tell us if he don't kill you?*

LAURIE *I knew something was wrong when he kept turning right, toward the*

130

river. When he pulled up at the warehouse I wanted to scream at him
THIS ISN'T MY BUILDING! But my throat was so dry! I
thought about yanking the door handle open and running, but then he
said he just wanted to check a tire, so I swallowed and waited. When
he climbed into the back seat I tried to scream but there was no one
around and he got his hand over my mouth so quickly! I could smell
cigarettes on his fingers. I scratched him and scratched him and then
he hit me, twice, with his open palm on the side of my head. I
couldn't see. I gave up. I kept trying not to think. He was so big. I
couldn't move. After he was still I opened my eyes, he wanted me to
see the knife before he used it. He must've stabbed me about twenty
times, I was dead before he pushed me out of the cab.

ANGELINA   *How come you let your wife come home so late by herself? In the old*
country men looked after their women. The worst thing is, I'll bet she
enjoyed it. And besides, she says as the kid begins to drift up-
wards, layers of landscape dissolve beneath him, *it's your dream.*
Momentarily he reaches up toward wakefulness and groggy,
tries to cry out, but before he can open his mouth he is dozing
again.

A quiet night at Tony's means only half the Counselor's boys
at the polished bar, amateurs ringing the pool table holler
for more chalk, couple of nurses on their dinner break order
Tony's special club sandwiches because the boys at the bar
always buy them beer and even a few hard ones which never
quite kill the smell off their uniforms. Four up-to-date licenses
taped to his fogged mirror. "Hey, Dutch! How's a boy?"

Nobody owns Tony. If he likes you, he'll carry you for a month,
maybe longer; you'll never find out why. You need bail money he
don't charge you 10 per cent, and he's got his own lines to the
precinct. But don't ever try to cross him. He ran an open house
straight through the thirties, Parisi's boys and the Glasser mob
made a deal at his back tables, but lots of little guys after a fast buck
are pushing concrete at the bottom of the river. Tony's a
survivor.

Off-nights he occasionally occupies a tiny back table with only
one chair, nobody offends by trying to join him. Nods affably
to new and older customers alike, fifteen years ago he stopped
drinking his own beer. He still gets high-priced ass, guaranteed
sanitary, without paying for it, and Anselmo's brother handles
his tax returns from an uptown office.

Chin resting on his crossed elbows Matto sniffed, swallowed,
lump compressing a tickle in his throat. No perfume. Parisi's
blonde only showed up three nights a week, he could never
remember which. "I'll buy you a beer," he managed once.
"Sure," she grinned, she could buy him and half the bar, but
accepted, clinked his glass and granted him a demure but
conspiratorial wink. A real lady. When she smiled and nodded
to him, because she could never remember what the boys

133

called him, he nodded back gravely while his groin throbbed.
Once at the rim of a crowd watching the pro finals he grazed
her tit with his elbow, but she didn't notice. He thought.
Spongy, resilient, the Swede girl had younger breasts easily as
big and never wore a bra; in the humid stable mornings during
milking she'd nip his ear when his scarred and callused hands
fumbled under her heavy sweater. Or her father's lumberjacket
she took for a cloak when she crept barefoot across the yard
to his cabin.

Father met Matto market day in Pendleton and stared at his
hands while Matto stammered an explanation of where he'd
worked, hired him as soon as Matto dried up, no questions
asked. Matto had learned another trade, one-family setups
where he hand-milked twenty cows twice a day and ranches
where with a dozen other hands he shepherded whole herds
through the milking machines. Bought grain, stored feed,
shifted straw, tended cracked hooves, assisted at calf births,
trucked giant milk jugs to market, spooned down thick bubbling oatmeal in white-washed bunkhouses. Winter the smell
from a wood fire curing bacon in a smokehouse carries miles
over snow, air so clear you can write your name with your
breath. Deep drifts marooned herds, blocked roads for the
season, every farm family did their snow-shopping early in Sep-
tember, huge tins of vegetables, fifty-pound slabs of butter,
once the radio announced all feeder roads blocked they froze
their milk and lived off the storehouse, pancakes every
morning, a thousand eggs and five hundred pounds of flour,
maybe it's monotonous but we sure as hell won't starve, boys.
Thick columns of smoke from the lower ridges signaled
giant steam plows chugging through drifts, they padded over

134

crusted surfaces to the boundary fence, only its tips showing, to watch the plows churn up the hills, stripping mountains of snow off the ribbon of black asphalt and slamming it into ridged barriers that imprisoned the road. Orange triangular pennant replaced the red flag flapping over the main barn as the big trucks revved up, ready to grind down-ridge to market again, fresh vegetables and a month's worth of mail and newspapers. Matto was always chagrined when a siege ended.

Spent thirty months working that spare terrain, longest stretch on the Swede's farm, wife and one sleepy daughter. Flat-fisted thud in the gray morning light on the slatted door of the shed they fixed up for the help, they offered Matto an alarm clock but he didn't trust himself to shut it off, jangling reminded him of air-raid sirens over Luzon, he hated to remember how much money he'd lost. Grunting, he shucked off the eiderdown and three khaki blankets, forced himself up into a shivering crouch, goatish in long underwear, groping for his clothes on the stove rack, ash still smoldering; on a really cold morning, twenty below, fire never lasted till morning. "Coffee's on, bub." When water froze overnight in the pipes, chunks of ice which he splintered into his washing-pan scraped his cheeks as he rubbed, crystals trapped in his beard dripped onto her oilcloth-covered kitchen table as he sipped her steaming coffee. They never expected him to shave, beards lasted all winter. Her kitchen was always warm, and she did all the toting, never asked for help with the coal and wood, even the morning he drove her down-ridge to hospital she had their coffee steaming on the hob. Neuralgia, they told her, but she knew better. He learned their talk. Single words

135

counted, a phrase was a speech, they left him alone but he never felt lonely. "More biscuits, son?" He put on weight, his shoulders straightened, gradually his body toughened until he could heave a fifteen-gallon jug onto a truck bed without straining to protect the scar tissue over his right ribs. He had a knack for gentling cows the Swede sensed in his hands the moment he saw him, couldn't raise his wages but offered him all the extras he could squeeze out of his own tight margins; a second day off every other month, a radio, curtains he didn't need for his shed's windows, the second-best cuts of meat and once a week his favorite pie for dinner and a whole extra one to take to his room. For once he stammered his thanks.

The Swede wanted him to stay, his wife understood Matto was the best hand they were ever likely to find. Matto wondered, afterwards, whether the Swede had prompted his daughter but decided he was too old-fashioned. They barely talked. The girl was eighteen, broad and big-muscled. Matto kept out of her way, no whores for hundreds of miles but he felt contained, clear mountain air. Work-weary, his flesh wanted only undisturbed sleep, his war years dropped away. "Why you always keep away from me?" she demanded. They occasionally rubbed shoulders as they cleaned the straw-matted aisles steamy with manure and animal heat. His muscles twitched at her touch. Her father called him a good man, deep, much gentleness, but Matto saw tall blond boys ride the school bus with her every morning, watched one of them jump off and, taking her hand, stray down the path along the south ridge which crosses the creek and skirts the old hay wagon. "I'm not your people," he mumbled. She stared at him, wordless, light off whitewashed walls glinting pale blue

136

in her eyes. Two mornings later, cows shifting stolidly in fresh
hay, she bit the loose skin of her wrist and seized his hand,
drops of fresh milk on her fingers, nipped him twice just below
the knuckles. "My teeth leave the same marks in your skin
as in mine." He tried to explain, excited but too fearful. She
was too good for him, her father paid his wages, all he knew
about were paid-for women. She stared at him fumbling for
words. That night she creaked open the door to his shed,
her father's lumberjacket slung like a cape over her coarse
flannel nightgown, knelt beside his bed so her face was level
with his own on his pillow. She folded his hand in hers and
kissed his knuckles, then sucked the tips of his fingers, he felt
the hard biting edge of her teeth just grazing his nails. "I am
a bad man for you. No good at all. I know only bad women.
You must go. What can I tell your father?" He promised himself to make her go but just to touch her hair he reached out for
her. She came almost every night, waiting at least an hour
after her father had blown out the bedroom candle and
pulled the heavy comforter over their mammoth double bed
before climbing out her bedroom window, she never dared
the doors which always creaked. She lay with him till the false
dawn, an hour before the first rooster crowed, then tiptoed
back on bare feet across the frozen mud of the yard. He was
her first, dark and lean while the others were fair-haired,
blockish; subtle curves to his limbs, scars he described in
whispers, fierce passion which exulted her whenever she provoked him, she was content. In the daytime she managed not
to touch him, they guarded themselves so carefully they
seemed, to the parents, hostile. Sullen and secretive. At meals
the mother served, the father said grace, Matto and the girl
mumbled hesitant amens. He stumbled like a sleepwalker into

137

a sudden riotous spring. Everything dripped, water poured down the upper slopes, mud caked his boots and denims, the lower paths flooded, they tended a harvest of wet-nosed, shaky calves. One night during supper the father confronted him. "You know that girl carries your child?" His mouth dry, wind caught in the double windows roaring in his ears, Matto nodded; she'd already told him. His ears turned red until he dropped his glance, across the table a slow flush stained her cheeks but she stared proudly at him. "You can marry in the church by the end of the month, no one will talk. You move into the guest room, there is already a double bed." Matto was incapable of shaking his head, he stared at his hands. "The farm can be yours, after us. After we go. No one else to keep it. You know how to take care of it, it would stay in good hands, for your children to belong to after you." That night he sweated in the cold spring air, pounded his knotted fist into his mattress, trying to find words. She understood only that he wouldn't stay and cried till morning, mopping her swollen face on her father's jacket sleeve in the doorway of his shed as he stumbled down the pitted path to the road, a new duffle bag slung over his shoulder, he was afraid to turn and wave a final goodbye because she might burst into tears again and wake her father.

"That one must be stale by now, Dutch. Try another one." Slopping stein shoved across the bar. And at Matto's disclaimer: "Don't worry about it, Dutch. It's on the house." Pursed lips, beer already swirling in his empty stomach, Matto nodded, a sandwich or one of Tony's quick steaks, thin shavings of meat with gristle to chew, but he wouldn't ask.

138

Needed to piss. Usually he forgot to pull the chain. Sweating pipes, moisture on peeling walls, shaky hand on cold radiator flanges propped him as he swayed. Somebody spat a soft curse from the pool table as a shot clinked home, sharp tap of impact and metallic slide as the ball slid through netting down the chute to its companions. Once he fell asleep on the hopper and they were about to bust the door in when somebody tried the knob which he never remembered to lock. "It's only Dutch." Reprieved, he shook his head, opened the door and limped into the corridor, watched Mauro bust his run with a carom which skittered off the bank and stopped three inches too short, somebody snorted as the tip of his stick tore felt. "You left your cane, Dutch." And a fresh stein waiting for him. Swallowed more of his pride, his stomach swilling. "You got some potato chips, Eddie?" Quick assessing glance. "Sure, Dutch. Lissen, I got something better, I got almost a whole cheese sandwich I been saving 'cause it's a shame to throw it out, Frankie's girl came in about five but all she could do was look at it after she ordered it, she didn't take more than a bite, she says she's definitely going to the hospital 'cause her stomach never gets any better. Hold on a second I'll give you some pickle to go with it."

Tired, but with some solid hunks of bread sopping the beer
in his stomach, he limped home. Joe would've stood him to
eggs or a bowl of chili but he preferred the warmth of Tony's,
even on an off-night. Familiar shapes, empty warehouses,
first spring drunks braving wet doorways, nobody ever
bothered to panhandle him. Twenty-five-cent hotels in 'Frisco,
Denver, Kansas City, smell of caked flesh, in 'Frisco a disease
he caught shipboard rotted his scalp, left his hair in handfuls
on the pillow when he woke, mornings.

*Alarm like a siren, bald-headed monster with a billy-club routs
you out by slamming iron bed rails, nine o'clock and the maid's
bucket which never kills the smells.*

Though he got discharged in Oakland, his records recorded
only the administrative reality, regional headquarters across the
Bay at the Presidio but since August the West Coast region
was handling six transports a week, average, GI's poured off
the ramps to be handed their discharge papers by an exhausted
trio of sergeants working around the clock, abbreviated *rites
de passage,* as their feet hit American soil for the first time
in four years a gruff voice grunted, "Here's yours, Mac,"
and they were civilians again. Matto stuffed his sheaf of papers
into his breast pocket and forgot them when he crammed his
uniform into a garbage can guarding the alley door of the
second-hand clothing store where he bought his first civilian
suit. "Great fit," little man chuckled, GIs bought anything
with lapels. "It was made for you." Wasted on Matto, who
glanced at himself in the streaked mirror and saw only his
pouched, heavy-lidded eyes. Poker shipboard, old Dutch
passenger liner refitted as a refrigerator ship by the Netherlands

141

Maritime Board, ill-fated experiment in Indonesian beef mercifully cut short by the Japanese. Reconverted into a troopship, tarpaulin stretched and weighted over tiled swimming pool, bunks for three hundred men but Matto and the steady poker hands traded for cots on the hardwood dance floor. Forced up on deck an hour a day by a jittery exec fearful of scurvy, for twenty-six days they played as close to nonstop as lax ship's drill and their bowels permitted. When they finally anchored off the Point, Bay area men yelling themselves hoarse at landmarks almost completely veiled by the thick fog blanketing the harbor, Matto was short approximately two hundred hours sleep and $5,700 out of the $6,000 he'd bankrolled from Balzano's liquor-supply operation plus accumulated regular pay. Balzano might've helped him salvage some of his dough but they split up in Luzon, Balzano wangled a transfer to a freighter bearing a Guam outfit packing $10,000 apiece, flyboys were easy pickings, deadly in a short game but over the long haul of a Pacific cruise he figured they trusted their instincts too much, the percentages would work his way. They did. He docked with $43,000, enough for his first three boats; when he finally pulled up in front of his mother's frame house in Catonsville he just clamped his hand on the horn of his '38 Pontiac and held it down till the whole neighborhood piled out. He picked it up in St. Louis, prices were cheap there, none of his style rubbed off on Matto.

Who dozed through his few good cards, misread his combinations, bet straight into traps, green waves dulling his eyes, shrill white birds, rare dorsal fins beckoning hundreds of bodies stripped to Army issue shorts to the rails as the watch's whistle signaled in the swimmers. Matto never braved the water.

Token evening breeze carried big-band music over AF short-wave, boomed to the decks through badly wired loudspeakers, occasionally a blues harmonica, mournful guitar. Women's handwriting crawled across already memorized sheets of crinkly paper, Matto stared at thumbed and faded photographs, mumbled appreciation. Three days off the coast they made him quit, tore up his IOU's and forked over $300 out of their winnings; angry at themselves for letting him play, knowing he was a simp, his money riding easy in their pockets, they decided no dogface could go home empty-handed. He sat on a life preserver, staring at the waves till they broke on a rock shore.

Home was one room four blocks away. Forced his knee joints to flex as he pivoted on his cane, avoiding puddles, figuring that in two days, three days, with a brace and liniment he'd work the trucks again. A Puerto Rican girl tight-busted in a lime-green sweater clopped past on teetery heels and straps which seemed to bind her ankles, she looked fourteen but was probably older, they all started young. As her thin heels retreated he wondered how many she'd already had and how much they'd paid; maybe once his knee was better he'd save up, the only Spics he'd had were south of the Canal, out of his tankers' wages. *She didn't cry but bit the pillow, after she mopped up her blood she waited for what else I wanted.* Aunt Carrie washed his uniforms twice a week, gagged at the smells, used Paregoric to settle her stomach. "Couldn't you find cleaner work?" Dominick signed him aboard the garbage scow, Matto knew she needed every cent for her own kids though she never begrudged him, and why put in yet another year trying

143

to pass eighth grade, nobody needed a high school diploma. Not for the jobs he could handle. "It ain't exactly the Navy, kid, but it's $35 a week plus eats and whatever you scrounge."

Truckers picked out the choicest stuff but saved what the bargemen wanted, Matto garnered a sheepskin-lined mackinaw and a heavy pair of lace-up lumberjack boots, only one sole gone. By dusk half the barges were loaded, tugs linked up a foursome while Matto's crew secured their chains, lose a hand in those links without blinking as each tug pulled a line taut, whistled in warning before the first lurch started a slow caravan downriver. Midstream their right of way, no maneuverability, on foggy nights the lead tug hooted continually, mournful warnings for in-shore tankers and vegetable barges hugging the breakwaters. Matto always nested on the Manhattan side, building a bunk from baled newspaper.

One night Dominick elbowed him awake off the Hook, pointing. "Lookit that, Dutch." Blackened hulk, drifting at anchor five hundred yards off the quays. Three tugs brought her in, derelict, burned up all her oil sixty miles off Hatteras, legend for weeks throughout the Sound, once they boarded her carboned decks they took off twenty charred bodies. "This here's our big chance," Dominick reckoned. "Lightning don't never strike twice, but all these long-haul men are superstitious as niggers. We'll get cards easy." So Matto became a full-fledged merchant seaman on the coffins of two dozen men expecting to retire at fifty; dead men's shoes, Aunt Carrie said, made a long face and shook her head. At dawn, after the barges docked, Dominick hailed a taxi downtown and they signed on, no questions asked, a thirty-day bonus and a fresh longshoreman's card with his own name typed in.

They skirted the straggling picket line, wives and mothers shrouded in black shawls demanding compensation specifically excluded in the contract, the company finally bought them off, pittance not worth bad publicity. "Scabs!" they screamed, but Dominick just shrugged his tired shoulders. "Those guys had this outfit sewed up so tight you couldn't borrow a lug wrench to change a tire unless you were somebody's brother-in-law."

Vera Cruz, Managua, San Cristóbal, Guayaquil, couldn't count in Spanish, used his fingers, saved his money. A gypsy fortune teller in Lima muttered as she bit his silver dollar. "This country is accursed. Death for Yanquis. You give your heart to an Indian girl she put a spell on you, wander barefoot for twenty years in the mountains, nobody find your grave." He kept his heart, hoarded his money, under Dominick's wing he bought his way through the cheapest houses, a one-night stand with a full bottle of raw Indian mash was cheaper than a good steak in a Hoboken tavern. The girls spoke only sailors' English, lexicon of curses, and Matto's hands were creased with rope burns and encrusted with oil. He got what he paid for.

Except once. Binge at a cat house top of the hill by the end of the cable car, last night before shipping out. Proprietor auctioned off her girls, saving the most delectable for last, copper-skinned sharp-jawed little princess, black flashing eyes. "The old bitch says she's only thirteen. And a virgin!" "Ah, it's bullshit! They're all on their backs by ten." Matto outbid his shipmates, twenty dollars bought her for the night. Stared at his hands in a cubicle narrow as his bunk while she undressed. High child's breasts, thin curling soft brown thatch,

145

quickly onto her back on straw pallet covered with worn
yellowed sheeting, her knees flexed, trying to smile up at him,
she'd been instructed. He sat. Perhaps he was tired. But twenty
dollars was a hell of a lot of money to waste on one night's
sleep beside a sullen little girl. He heaved himself aboard the
cot, kissed her forehead, covered her with a thin blanket
folded at the foot of the pallet and, stripping off his faded
corduroys and black pullover, slipped in beside her. But he
couldn't sleep. He held her, traced her thin-boned back with
his scarred hands, fondled her breasts and buttocks and fingered
her slit as she nipped his neck. He anchored her, tiny breasts
squashed against his undershirt and his forefinger grazing
her clit, shyly she sang to him, nuzzling his ear, gradually
they drifted into a cramped sleep. He awoke to a chorus of
roosters, morning sun already hot, throbbing erection. She
was pillowed away from him, coarse damp hair shielding her
eyes, thumb in her mouth. Wedged himself ready to thrust, as
he circled her waist and grasped her shoulders she woke,
twisted to stare at him over her shoulder. He drove again and
again, barely noticing her biting her pillow to stop her screams,
her small breasts made slippery handholds. After he withdrew
she lay, staring at the wall, then rolled off the pallet. Pool of
blood staining the straw, on board he nodded when they asked
about whether he got his money's worth. He dressed quickly,
tossed an extra silver dollar onto the pallet before he shuffled
out. Half the crew was already drinking coffee at the low
courtyard tables, but he didn't satisfy their curiosity.

Cursed his knee up all four flights of stairs, nobody remembered hearing him. They entered his key on the blotter, plus one handkerchief, $1.42 in change in a worn cloth purse with both catches broken, and one marble. Actually an agate shooter, cops have bad memories. Draped his soggy pants on the radiator, arranging the creases, not that the feeble morning heat would manage much steam-pressing. He slept in his underwear, on the farm she'd bought him two pairs of flannel pajamas which he'd chuckled to wear, pleased and warmer, though they itched. But he left them behind. For the next man? Water too cold to wash in, Aunt Carrie hated smelly sheets, he rinsed his mouth and eased himself into bed, shifting on the lumpy mattress till his throbbing knee found a ridge to brace on.

Tug from the harbor, mournful, at the crest of its hill the Home was a cemetery, creepers marred her name. "You look so much older! And your uniform—I can't get over it." She didn't expect him, all he sent were some postcards, did they print what he told them to? Balzano did, three of the others got it, Terry with a bullet in his mouth which tore off the back of his head. They call her Carmelita here, the girl at the desk laughed when he asked for Aunt Carrie. "It's not so bad. The other women are so old and decrepit, they sleep all day! Me, I went for walks so much they told me to join the Boy Scouts. Then my veins started." She patted her thick ankle, Matto's knee throbbed, her calves bulged out of thick-webbed medical stockings, strangled blue veins. "I stay off my feet. They call me the sentry, I ride this rocker every day it doesn't rain." And none of the children came, Geracimo's two sons and a daughter. "Geracimo stayed like a corpse on his back, we joked

147

about him, did he ever sleep? Here the old women sit and wait, footsteps in the night, in the morning nurses tell us, Mrs. So-and-So had to go away. You were always a good boy, your mother would be proud of you. Better she lived than me like this. Promise you'll light a candle for me, nobody else will. I wish I could walk you to the station, but it's too far."

Geracimo could swallow and slide his tongue but his jaws opened only wide enough for a spoon. Matto held the basin as her blue washcloth sopped puddles of suds, she scoured the crevices of Geracimo's balls as methodically as his armpits and the hollows of his shoulders; after he wet himself his urine dried and collected, sour scabby flakes, in the crinkles and hair of his genitals. Then they both heaved him gently over so she could scrub his back and rump, corkscrewing her cloth to probe his ass-hole. Matto's job to soap his feet which, useless, were always clean; they bathed him three times a week, to keep him feeling fresh, Aunt Carrie said, she took Geracimo's blink for approval. Matto hated soaping between his toes. Old scales, clammy under his fingers, he tried to hold his breath to keep their odor from moiling his stomach. "Don't make such faces! I told you, you're imagining it. They don't smell!"

Once he woke to a swelling under Geracimo's thin coverlet. Crept to bedside, too fearful to glance at Geracimo's face, tugged till the coverlet slid off his uncle's middle. Through the unbuttoned slit of his uncle's fly his prick, taut, erect, sick milky white, protruded, twitching, only moving member in Geracimo's body. No grin wrinkled his uncle's cheeks, did his eyes blink more rapidly? Too confused to be certain, Matto stared until his uncle subsided. A few days later he began to miss his turn keeping watch, too slow to find excuses. They

148

stopped asking him, Geracimo was only his uncle not his father, and if he didn't care enough—Aunt Carrie shrugged her shoulders. "Nobody holds it against you."

Shawl. "He's gone now," nodding her head. "I would like to go home. Take me home." Taking his hand, they tiptoed across a salt beach, crystals smoking in the sun. "When my health was bad I soaked here," and ripped off her leg bandages to frolic, petticoated, in a boiling sea. *You forgot the beach ball.* "Come in," she shrieked, dimpling, water molding her striped suit. "I always forgot you were such a good boy. You don't even know how to kiss your aunt." Stunned by the bite of her nails he plunges after her, fisherman's boots to his knees melt in blazing sand, oily footprints stained by the tide, he slithers into the sea. Wet hand on her knee slides up to her gash where she clamps him, under her plastic transparent umbrella her little girl boobs are lemon pips, she winks at him as she twirls her parasol and saunters into the sun, *when it rains it pours.* As he drifted into a deeper sleep first morning light touched his grimy window.

Hot towels plastered his cheeks, blood wiped onto tissue paper. "Need a wire cutter for those whiskers." Guilliano, Dominick, the Counselor's boys, and even Mr. Amato from the bank, all smelling of mint, rosewater. "You kids leave that chair alone." Reserved for the Counselor, who rested his bulk in its worn leather, dropping cigar ash, and swivels, lathered, to face his realm. "You thought we forgot about you, but all along we been watching." Kneeling, he accepts his investiture, Cinelli's cane taps his shoulder, he rises Sergeant-at-Arms, Parisi's blonde tongues his ear and squashes his badge against her breasts. Moist for him. "Come, come, please come." As

149

he kneels, extended, dry-mouthed, dazed in gray morning light, his callused hands stroke his swelling and he burrows away from the window, drifts through eels and squashed beer cans, cobblestones, Gianfredo's uncle cranks his hurdy-gurdy and a monkey in porter's cap dances to a scatter of coins, he flicks a silver dollar into its quick paws on one bounce as the crowd gasps in admiration. Her hip grazes him, sweat staining the armpits of her dress, "Come on, Dutch, give us a break! Give us a try for old time's sake." He shoves his marker into the only vacant space on the checkered board. As the wheel spins she nips his ear, leather thong clacks over pins as the wheel slows, *thack thack thack thack*, one bushel basket heaped with coins at his feet, the second basket on his number as the wheel whirls again. "Hurry, hurry!" she whispers, a team of black horses is hitched to a wagon weighted with bushels of coins, blacksmiths hammer their traces, *clang clang clang clang*. The wheel spins, hammer pounding spikes, he hoists her into the stirrups. "Now. Now!" They gallop through packed streets, shower of coins as he empties each wagon, metal slams onto cobblestones *clang clang clang clang* he wakes with a pounding head. Three feet from his stiff left arm his radiator vibrates and bellows at his room. Gropes for his trousers and barefoot follows the clanging into the dark hallway and upstairs to shove through her unlocked door and limp into her kitchen where she flails wildly at her cold radiator flanges with the flat base of her blackened frying pan. With the only pure motion of his life he sweeps the pan's handle from her startled fingers and swings it through an arc which, completed, smashes her skull.

150

Jerked upward, blinking, whose eyes on me? Shaky hand crept to his scrotum, cupped. Gray light, whose curtains? Shivering he lets his head sag back onto her pillow, Angelina propped on her elbow, staring. Grunted, shook his head. "Must've hit bottom again. Last thing I remember something was trying to take my head off, tentacles poking the inside of my skull."

She nodded but didn't touch his extended arm. "You talk a lot in your sleep. All mumbles. And you grind your teeth like mad!"

Yawned, then stared up at her through slow fingers rubbing at his eyelids. Bound to be edgy. We got maybe three hours sleep and I had an extra hour while she tangled with Sal. "Hey! Today's Sunday! Nikky doesn't have school today, we can sleep."

"You tell her that. She runs on the same clock, seven days a week. And anyway, she's got Catechism today. Class starts at eight thirty, I already made her breakfast. We both been up almost an hour, I only came in to see how the hell you could sleep through all our racket."

His hand, wriggling through the tangle of sheet toward her thigh, intent on stroking then rubbing up the small of her back to ease her weary muscles, froze, beat a quiet retreat back to nest between his thighs, warming. "It's that Marsala I bought, it turned to vinegar in my stomach. I'm afraid even to belch, I can feel it bubbling up."

Still she stared past him, focused somewhere over his head at the patterned bedroom wall. "My stomach's on the fritz, too, I'm gonna have the trots before lunch, I can feel it. Thank God her class lasts three hours."

151

Reprieved! He stroked himself, reassured. With another three hours I can get my head cleared again, might even attempt another tumble before Nikky bursts in covered with holy water. Or don't they sprinkle them in Catechism? A couple more hours' sleep, Angie, and I could be a hell of a lot more sympathetic. Pushed himself up, nauseous lurch of his stomach spun his balance and tilted the room and her drapes sideways, sliding. "Jesus!" and grabbed for the headboard. Slowly the room righted. "I gotta go take a piss, get some cold water on my forehead, rinse my mouth out. I'll be right back. I think." Crawled past her to the foot of the bed, padded on shaky feet to her bathroom and squinted through the open slit of her bathroom window at a trio of cars racing lights up the Avenue. As he shook himself dry he realized he was starting to swell. Good old incorrigible, nothing keeps him down. They'll probably bury me with an erection. What if I just marched in with my rod sticking out and told her that what we both needed was another tumble? Suppose I didn't say anything, just walked in and put it to her? Flushed the toilet, grinning, and sidled back to her bedroom, shielding himself as he tunneled under her sheets. She was still slumped at the foot of her bed, staring out her narrow window, one of her heavy drapes yanked partially open to expose the airshaft. Weak light blurred the pits under her eyes, when she turned back to him she looked less troubled, softer.

"I'd better go make sure Nikky's dressed decent. Those sisters are eagle-eyed, they never miss nothing."

Her slippers flapped down the hallway to Nikky's room, his flesh still rigid under his hand. It's natural she's edgy, they been together too long. Like she always says, neither of them are

152

kids any more. Surprising Sal lost his cool, no point getting touchy at his age. Yawned and squirmed onto his stomach, his swelling pinned under his soft belly flesh. Come back in here, Angie, just come back and slide into bed. She's not coming back. By now she's probably got Nikky out the door and she's sitting by the kitchen table staring out the window. Maybe she's even curled up on Nikky's bed, there's no hope for me till she gets some sleep. A hot shower's what I need, a hot shower and then a cold shower. And then a hot shower, a hot shower with Angie pinned against the steamy shower door, soap her up good till she's lathered and wriggling and then get it into her from behind, my head up to take the water in fine spray on my forehead, my face, open my eyes wide to let it wash my eyeballs. Quick footsteps down the hallway and Nikky padded in and punched at him curled under the sheets, he heard her giggle as her tiny balled fists poked for his ribs and crotch. Head shielded beneath Angie's pillow, he stroked himself and imagined Nikky's compact body twisting as he rolled over to seize and haul her in, wriggling prize still damp from the washrag scrubbing Angie always administered, spirited her under her mother's sheets and guided her willing head down to his swollen crotch. Squinting to capture Nikky's moist little mouth, feverishly licking, he came, sopping himself with a corner of Angelina's sheet, quick spasms, heat immediately replaced by calculation, his glop pooling sticky puddles on her linen. Embarrassing evidence. Avoiding the splotches he edged onto his side, two hours' sleep and it might dry. Meanwhile Nikky's pummeling continued, clearly Catechism could wait. He played possum, occasionally groaned, shifting when a chance blow found softness to prod. Finally Angelina yelled for Nikky from the kitchen, he listened to her retreating foot-

153

steps as he sopped up the most concentrated pools and spread the rest across her sheet, heard Nikky slam the door. Dampness on his thighs as he drifted. Her hairbrush clinking onto her hand mirror woke him, she was already dressed.

"Jesus, I went under again! Why didn't you wake me up? The last thing I remember is Nikky punching me in the ribs. As well as a couple other places." Propped himself up, hugging his knees, he blinked at her, groped with his left hand. The sheet was crinkled and stained but almost dry.

"I went out. I just got back. I didn't feel like bothering to wake you."

Stared past the back of her head to meet her eyes in her mirror. "That was ambitious for a Sunday morning. Where'd you go?"

"I walked Nikky to church. Then I walked up to the Square and sat and looked at the kids jammed around the fountain. Then I had some coffee. Those kids must get to the fountain awful early. When I was a kid we stayed home Sunday mornings. I seen both of Malafronte's girls, the older one was picking at a guitar with her head resting on some spade's shoulder. If her mother'd seen that, she woulda had a stroke. It's been years since I went to the Square. Musta been a thousand kids. Nikky'll hang out there when she gets a little older." He could see her eyes shift to focus on him. "Lissen, I think we should call it quits."

He let his mouth fall open. Now come on, this is exactly what you were expecting. But he couldn't fight his panic, stomach churning and a quick pulse beating at his temples. "Huh?" he said, once he was sure of his voice. "What are you talking

154

about?" She wriggled around on her dressing stool till she was facing him, she wasn't angry. "I just wanna know one thing before—" dismissal, a decisive wave of her right hand. "Not that I expect a straight answer. But what'd you expect to get out of this? Why'd you start up with me in the first place, just for a little action? You never laid nobody from the neighborhood before?"

"What do you mean?"

"Whatta you mean, what do I mean? I wanna know what you think you're doing here. I wanna know what it means to you. I'm just another piece of ass, right? Maybe it's more kicks for you, screwing me three floors downstairs in your own building?"

Deep breath, shaking his head. "Now hold it. We had a bad night, right? We drank too much and we all got angry with each other and maybe we even made love too much." He couldn't manage the phrase without hesitating to cover his wince, he wondered if she noticed. "Sal walks out and you get upset, and then you get almost no sleep before Nikky wakes up. Now you're angry at me, okay, and maybe you got good reasons. But I'm really tired." I need some coffee bad, sitting across from her at her kitchen table with a coffee cup steaming under my nose, I could pull my head together. Tried to grin. "You caught me with my pants down."

Her stool scraped as she pushed herself up. "I don't wanna *talk* about it. Just put your pants on and get out of here."

Waited until she slouched into the kitchen before flipping the blankets back to scramble out of bed. Dressing, he tried to steady his hands, you don't need her, for god's sake relax.

155

Throat dry and his stomach churning, he tried to consider why he was so frightened. Must be my hurt pride. Nobody's ever kicked me out before, I've only been with her a few months. He stared at his bloodshot eyes in her bathroom mirror. Surely she's too tough to want me to tell her how much I care? She just wants to get rid of me to make sure that Sal can walk back in here whenever he wants. But if Sal's so important, why shuffle between beds? I'm certainly not the world's most accomplished stickman, but then neither is Sal, at least from the looks of things. But that's not the point "Well, what the hell *is* the point?" he snapped, exasperated, then stared at the tightly wedged bathroom door, hoping his voice hadn't carried. Cold water splashing his face began to clear his head. He spent a long time combing his hair before he tousled it.

"Can I have some coffee before I go upstairs?" And when she shrugged but didn't turn to face him: "If you've still got some left in the pot, I could use some. There won't be anything but instant upstairs."

"Help yourself," she muttered from the window. "Take the whole pot upstairs if you want to. Just get the hell outa here!"

He poured his cup carefully, an undercurrent in her voice decided him he could risk pushing her. "Look, Angie, I'm not trying to say it does any good to talk, but you can't just kick me out like this."

"Bullshit I can't."

"Okay. You can if you want to. But it doesn't make any sense. That night on the roof was over three months ago, how many times have we seen each other since then? Ten? Maybe a dozen?

156

And each time it's been you worrying about Nikky or else wondering whether there's a chance Sal might take a half-hour off and decide to drop by, and me tiptoeing back upstairs wondering whether Laurie believes my story. It's not easy to get close to somebody under that kind of tension. You just can't get up one morning and blow the whistle because things aren't happening as fast as you want them to."

She let her shoulders sag as she turned from the window to slump into her chair. "I'm not looking for any soul mate. I just feel used, that's all, and I'm tired of it. Before Sal came there was just Nikky and every once in a while somebody I liked enough to take a chance with, a single woman with a kid in this neighborhood gets hustled plenty, everybody thinks she's an easy lay. I watched you for a long time, almost from the time you moved into this building, and I was curious; you were the first ones from outside the neighborhood ever moved in here, I wanted to know what you were like, how you were different from us. And I liked you, I liked the way you grinned and how soft your voice was, you always said something to make me laugh when I met you on the stairs. And sure, I wanted to screw you. But I was angry at myself the morning after that night on the roof. You probably didn't notice, but I thought it was my fault we rushed into bed so fast I never even tried to talk to you. But it's not my fault, I've tried plenty since then and you just brush me off. I'm just another cunt, that's all you want. You're tired of your wife and you thought you'd sample the action downstairs."

"Angie, it's not true." I thought you could take care of yourself, I thought I didn't have to pay that kind of attention. You come on so tough! I thought we were both in it for ourselves,

157

surely you didn't want a *relationship*? Both of us have been through enough to screw without complications. "I guess what I wanted was too simple. I mean, you had Sal. I didn't mean to come between the two of you."

"I'm not worried about Sal. Ever since Nikky was born I've been careful, I know what most of them want. I had Nikky because I wanted to, and bringing her up decent was always more important to me than being anybody's piece of ass. With a ring or without a ring. I moved back here because I knew the neighborhood and I knew I could manage. Sal was some kind of bonus. But you interested me, I thought you were different. I never even left the city, practically, and two years of technician's school on top of high school is everything I know, I don't even bother reading the papers. The worst thing is, I'm so ashamed." She was at the window again, yanking the curtains aside. "So you get out. I put up with you long enough, I don't have to cry in front of you." And when he didn't move: "I said get out."

Still tone which barely carried her words, but he was on his feet. He paused at the door, wanting to ask her to think it over. Pointless. He closed her door carefully behind him and started up the stairs to his apartment.

5:37–6:14
april 8, 1965   Baker's delivery truck ground gears as it squealed around a corner. The drivers he remembered, stacks of fresh loaves in cardboard trays against a padlocked doorway, were dead, their bread immune now in cellophane. Later he would mumble he lost his last shooter in the mud, but cops rarely take notes. A gypsy palm reader in Guayaquil, toothless, brass loops dangling from small scarred lobes, shook her head over his palm and refused his silver dollar, he didn't know how to make her tell what she'd seen. "Bad country for you," she mumbled instead. "Give your heart to an Indian girl, she keep you running for years. Bad blood, curse on your heart." He kept his heart and dragged his knee through eight rainy seasons, blood caked the base of her frying pan but the handle was clean except for the prints, his and a dozen others. As he neared the river the faded knife scar under his right ribs throbbed, he welcomed its reminder that his score was settled. Leaning against a pillar he watched miniature waves slap scum against rotting pilings. When they questioned him all he could remember was the luncheonette. *I wanted coffee so I went to Joe's like every morning.*

159

Joe's windows sweat in the hottest weather, and not because
he doesn't wash off the grime twice a week, after he lugs in his
milk cartons but before the first truckers arrive for breakfast,
with his bucket and squeegee he does a better job than anyone
he'd pay and besides he lives by cutting overheads, *on my
margins neon's a luxury.* Usually it drizzles before noon, thin
gray film coats the fruits of his labor so he expends ritual
curses and grants a sour grin to whoever's lounging at his
counter. Licencing Department's records say he's been on that
corner since '37; when he dies the soda company would reclaim
his billboards, fountain equipment, and grill, the ice-cream
firm would haul away his freezers. "Hiya, Dutch. Little early
this morning, ain't you?"

Usually Matto nodded, nobody expected more. "I got up
early," he said this time. "Specially." And thought about it.
"Good morning." Gravely. "How you feel today?"

If Joe was surprised he didn't show it, always tired in the
mornings, forced to open an hour earlier than anybody else
to catch the truckers. "I'm awright. Little tired." Maybe Joe
glanced at him and returned to scraping his griddle, solidified
grease which cracked and hardened no matter how clean he'd
scrubbed it closing time the night before. Matto swung himself gingerly onto a protesting stool, bracing his bad knee.
He always limped, Joe told the cops, *I didn't notice anything
special.* Drained off a mug of fresh coffee and set it before
Matto, shoving a plastic milk pitcher next to the sugar, never
remembered Matto drank his coffee black.

Cupped both hands around his mug before sipping and
shivered, though the sun was high enough now and Joe was

161

already damp under his T-shirt and worn white apron. "I would like two eggs, fried but turned over so the yellow don't run. And bacon. And two pieces of toast, with butter." Joe must've turned from the griddle to stare at him. "And when I finish, another cup of coffee. What kind of pie you got?"

Joe set himself to frying a perfect pair of eggs, occasion he dimly sensed, felt constrained to chatter. "Dutch, you still living in the same place, across the street from Tommy's?" A nod. "How'sa work going?" Another nod. "I seen Al out on the Island coupla weeks ago, with a whole gang of guys from Jersey City. He works at a packing plant across the river, made foreman easy. You remember Al, you worked with him on the night crew, I remember it was only two weeks before that fathead squealed we made a deal I'd have your eggs ready by the time you got down the hill, Al used to drop you off here every morning."

Matto nodded, staring at his eggs' filmy white edges spattering as fat sizzled on the black grill. "Yeah, I remember him." Was more demanded? He sighed, hunching his shoulders. "How is he?"

"I'm telling you, Dutch, he looked as good as I ever seen him! I asked him how he was making out and he said great, getting outa New York was the best thing happened to him. He don't miss nothing, not even the money, he's pulling in plenty without working nights. Or overtime." As Matto nodded, immersed in his browning eggs, Joe told a curious lie. "He asked about you. He asked about Jeff and Herman and then he wanted to know how you were doing. I told him you were making out okay."

162

"They're done." Matto pointed at his eggs. Joe shrugged, turned back to his griddle, whisked Matto's eggs onto a heavy white platter with a quick flip of his spatula, he'd fried an extra strip of bacon without expecting Matto to notice.

Matto stared at the diminishing whites of his eggs and chewed each mouthful, using his cup of lukewarm coffee to wash his toast down. Joe forgot Matto's second cup of coffee and finally forgot Matto until Matto wiped his sticky mouth with a corner of napkin and cleared his throat. "You should call them at the precinct. Tell him she's in the kitchen, on the floor. Tell them I wait here."

While they were waiting Joe saw a crumpled dollar bill by Matto's cup. "'I got some change if that's not enough,' he said, and then he said that the eggs were almost the way he liked them and then he thanked me. I told him it was on the house and then I yelled at him until he put the bill back in his pocket, what the hell else could I do?"

163

"I guess there wasn't as much work as he thought, he wanted to get out of that office so bad he kept overestimating. And finishing the job haunted him, he kept magnifying how hard it would be and how long it would take. But once we got out to his place he just let go, I could feel the tension drain out of him. By Saturday breakfast that sick greenish tinge around his jowls was gone, he could actually sit down and begin to work. Melanie kept pattering in to make us sample some shortcakes and biscuits she'd baked, both of us shooed her away and kept on working. We worked straight through dinner, he churned out sketches one after the other, we finished all the overlays by six thirty and then we decided to keep working so I could get home. He was so grateful to me, just for helping him get out of that office! He drove me to the station, I caught the midnight and pulled into Grand Central about 2 a.m. I should've called, but I wanted to surprise you, so I took a cab straight home."

Pinstripe blouse open on her smooth thin-corded neck, face above her cold coffee cup composed to contain an anxiety which kept breaking through into her glance. Quick sideways glances, confused, pain she's yielded to makes her vulnerable and she tolerates it, puffy eyes catching mine. Almost, for an instant, a plea. Then her lashes drooped, she glanced down at her spoon, a chipped nail, a noisy bus chugging into the Avenue, spoiling a quiet Sunday. She probably stayed awake, worrying, weighing the probabilities; she could've telephoned but she hates apologizing to people she's awakened. So he took a chance. "What time did you finally get in? You should've called me at Diebenborn's, his current girl went to sleep but the two of us talked until almost dawn. And even if we were asleep, what's one phone call?" Shrugged, pleased at his non-

165

chalance. "They'd just go right back to sleep again. I only stayed there out of laziness, he had some decent grass and I felt a little too wobbly to walk home. And afterwards we drank some of his Jamaica rum. Finally I just flopped on his floor and fell asleep; when I woke up one of his Mexican rugs was covering me. His girl must've got up early and figured I'd get cold. I stink, I sweated like crazy underneath it and then it shed all over me. Mexicans must weave their rugs out of dog's hair."

Overplayed? No way to tell. Took him full fifteen minutes to climb the three flights separating his apartment from Angie's, but once he reached his landing he'd regained enough control to notice his door ajar, ridge of telltale white paint exposed inside his sill. Calculation his nerves knew was unnecessary as he groped for his key. Laurie! Leaning against the peeling hallway wall, relief flooded him. Now it's really over. Mopping her damp cheeks with a corner of pillowslip, snuffling through a clogged nose because she's cried all night, he considered the terms of his confession, where blame should be apportioned. Confident, he folded his key back into its plastic case, we can start all over again. But you don't want to. That reedy current deep inside his head, idly he wondered what would disconnect it. Anyway, she'll take the blame on herself first, flicker of satisfaction twisted his grin, I hope she's had at least as bad a night. She knew nothing for certain, how he chose to play it would determine her response. Then this is hardly the time to contemplate major ruptures, right? And you can't stand out here all afternoon, considering. We go on as if nothing had intervened until I know what I want. However that comes about. Resolved, he shoved his door open and marched into his hallway. "Laurie? Laurie!" he shouted, pleased at the gen-

166

uine surprise in his tone. "What're you doing home so early? Harrison get another attack?"

Staring down at the empty Avenue from his front window, he felt her eyes bead on him as he bent over the cold radiator. Far below some four blocks west the river was slate-gray, tiny slice of water penned between warehouses and dock. She wants some kind of reassurance and she's ashamed to ask, moreover she suspects the distance between us is greater than she knows how to bridge. He could sense her building up to say something and was tempted to turn, stare till she backed down or swallowed her words, but instead he kept his back to her and tried to stare at the river.

"I thought—on the phone, when I called from the office, I thought you would be angry. At least annoyed with me, for spoiling your weekend. And then I was so pleased when you weren't, I felt like a child handed a present completely by surprise, only afterwards I realized how prepared I'd been for your surliness. I brooded on the train, the more I realized how relieved I'd been, the more depressed I got. We've gotten so far away from each other, it took this thing with Harrison to make me realize the awful bondage I'm locked into. I spend most of my energy avoiding you, trying to make sure I don't do anything to displease you. I've given up hoping anything good happens between us, I'm just trying to avoid disasters. And the worst part is, I didn't even know it was happening, I've just been functioning like a little robot. It was only once I got back here and found you weren't in that it occurred to me why you weren't angry on the phone, and then I just collapsed. It made so much sense, such perfect sense, I couldn't understand why it's taken me all these months to realize you had another woman!"

167

"Laurie." She was hunched over their dining table, both elbows propping her hands cupping her chin. He could tell she'd cried herself out; a rare state for her, lucidity. "Laurie." Softly. "I'm sorry. I'd have left a note, where you could call me, but—I just had no idea. Given all the times I've stayed out all night and you haven't worried—"

"But don't you see it doesn't make any difference even if you weren't with somebody else? Maybe you should've been! Don't you understand what I felt?"

She was staring without focusing at the indifferent grain of the table top, once carefully restored through hours of hand-sanding and the application of countless coats of varnish remover, but now badly scarred by pot scalds and coffee stains she'd long ago given up trying to remove. How long since she'd debated mending the curtains which trailed their loose hems across their floorboards and then chose, instead, an afternoon movie without his prompting? "That things were dead between us," he said finally.

"And that we were living out some kind of crazy ritual, a collusion in which both of us pretended that everything was perfectly okay so that we could go on doing—doing what? Doing what we always did! Don't you see, what are we protecting? We're not even doing anything that we care about!"

His heels banging the radiator shield kept time to the slow whine of the ventilator across the airshaft, turning on the slight breeze. "It's not quite that bad."

"Oh, look!" Flash of animation as she waved her hand at him, a quick flare of impatience which brought momentary color to her cheeks. "It's pretty bad, we don't have to fight about exactly how far apart we are. I've caught myself at least four times since we went on summer office hours, redoing a sketch I knew would pass, just because another two hours at the board would get you into bed and sleepy enough so you'd only mutter and turn over when I finally got in. I hate that job so much sometimes, it's not even busywork, my hands get so lumpish they feel like those wooden block wedges you shove into shoes to keep the leather from creasing. The third time I realized what I was doing, I was so guilt-stricken I ruined my sketch and took a cab home, determined to make it up to you. But you were tired. You apologized very formally for being so tired. I was very upset, I was all set to confess to you what I'd caught myself doing. I felt very tender toward you, and open. But you didn't even notice. And since you pretend not to notice how late I get in these days, I never bother to explain. We've both stopped noticing how many days go by when we never touch each other at all, I gird myself to kiss you good morning, you nod at me like I've just passed the sugar. And underneath all the coolness I feel this mammoth resentment from you, beating at me, shoving me into a corner. What're you trying to do to me, for god's sake, why are you trying to destroy me?"

She hid her head in her arms but he could hear her sobbing, knew it was impossible to cross the room to her, touch her hair or take her hand. "You know that's not right—you know that's a crazy thing to say. You know I'm not trying to destroy you."

"I don't know what I know any more." Though her face was buried he could hear her clearly. "I can't even think! And I don't understand anything about where you are—it just feels to me like you hate me!"

169

He considered their two shelves of records, the hi-fi he'd assembled badly, cursing the ambiguous instruction sheet, the frayed oriental rug they'd salvaged from a country auction, delighted at the price. "I don't hate you." Realizing it was, at least, accurate. "At least get that out of your head. It doesn't help anything. I don't hate you. I don't even believe that's what you really feel."

She wiped her runny nose with the heel of her hand, staring at the hanging plant she still managed to water. "Maybe it's just the word. Hostility. Anger. And an immense coldness, which I feel you taking pleasure in. I feel like you're trying to get back at me in some way. I feel you paying me back. Sometimes I feel you're getting your revenge for something I'm not even aware I've done."

He let her stare, pacing himself, the first quivers of uneasiness stirring in his stomach. "You know that hostility," he said. "And you've always known, it's just that when the pressure gets really intense inside me I can't contain it, I take another target and project some of what I'm feeling. You know why I turn it on you. I'm sorry for my tone but it's the same ground we've gone over a hundred times before. I've been going out of my skull for six months but what the hell's the point of trying to tell you, you'd only try to console me with that pat-pat way you have, which either makes me feel condescended to or else makes me realize you don't have the slightest real feeling for what I'm trying to tell you, why the hell shouldn't I keep it to myself? I've almost quit about four times these last months, did you maybe guess that? Or did you think things were going just fine at the old Center? Okay," he said as she made a motion to deny it, aware he'd actually been yelling,

"I admit that's unfair, you've known work hasn't been going well. But did you figure I'll probably be unemployed before long? Carson had me on the mat the other day because my reports have been falling off, I started out writing essays and now what I hand in's barely literate. She was being kind; in fact, I've stopped handing in reports. I can't manage to write them, I can barely manage to get on that goddam subway and head uptown, and I've skipped my last three days in the field completely. It's only a question of time till she has to fire me."

"You could quit. You've been beating your brains out for two years now and if there isn't any more point to doing it, you could just quit. You know why you went to work there and it hasn't worked out, how much longer do you have to put in your time before you can leave honorably? It's another one of those private notions you have, nobody's keeping score. Marvin quit after only nine months and nobody accused him of not sticking it out long enough. And besides," she said, reluctantly, he had the sense of his words slowly over-running what she'd wanted to say, "if you're really going to get fired, it makes more sense to quit now, why wait for Carson to fire you? You quit now and Carson can probably cover you for full unemployment. And anyway you don't have to work at all if you don't want to, we can get along easy with what I bring home."

And subsided, wearily. Slumped back against the ladder-backed Shaker chair rescued from her grandmother's farm, her hands cupped on the table.

"And do what?"

She was still staring at her hands. "I don't know," she said, "but then how would I know when you don't know? All I know is all the answers you'd give to anything I suggested. I don't pretend to know what the ways out are, I just know Welfare's a blind alley and there's no point getting fired because you're not prepared to quit. But you know you should quit, you've known for months you'd have to quit, now you're arranging to have yourself fired instead of quitting which is just stupid, it messes up your record. Why don't you just quit and I'll work overtime for a few months while you're collecting unemployment and we'll save enough to get out of here!"

"You mean this place?" He was too startled by her rush of words to think quickly, her cheeks flushed now, her eyes had lost their despairing glaze. "No, not here. Not just this place. I mean the city, the East Coast, all of it. I started to think about it when we were chugging up toward Harrison's, all those terrible small Hudson towns, each one surrounded by its junkyards and its old factories and its new industrial parks—they're building a new Thruway extension right through his neighbor's field. I felt the same way coming back last night, watching those endless strings of roadway lights crawling back from the Hudson up into the hills. Let's get out. We've got no real ties here. I won't even miss this apartment once we've left it, I don't care about it any more. I've just let it run right down."

"I've noticed." Relieved, anger tempted him. You think changing places somehow helps, geography as an alchemy? Will the West Coast transform me, plug me into something I can't find here, make the two of us bloom again? Well, I suppose it's happened. Or appeared to. "I'm tired of this place, too. I don't even give a damn any more how much dirt piles up, if it wasn't for the stink I'd let the garbage rot in the kitchen instead of lugging it downstairs. The roaches even crawl across the mirror while I'm shaving because they know I won't bother to squash them any more."

She was standing now, tapping the smooth knobs of her chair with her long thin fingers. Soon she'd cross the room to stroke his head and run her fingers through his hair. "You could go back to graduate school. You could apply to Stanford or any of the schools in the Bay area, they'd all accept you. I could find work out there easily, even if you didn't get a grant we wouldn't be living badly."

For an instant before he dismissed it, the possibility conjured up a set of images he was ashamed to find pleasurable: semi-circle of sling chairs around a benign professor, musty quietness of library tombs, morning walks across damp grass. Texts to disembowel, reading list to traverse like a country, schedule of papers that shaped the formless months which stretched before him. Real toads in imaginary gardens. How can she expect I'll see going back to school as anything but a defeat? "We could settle somewhere in the Mission district, Dieben-born says houses are getting cheap there again, his sister's think-ing of going out. Even if I was at Stanford, it's only an hour's drive. Less, with the freeways. If we got a place high enough we could watch the fog roll in off the Bay. We could climb Tamalpais again."

"I could see Monica. And Mike, and Robin and Ann. If I wrote to Ann she might even find me a job so I could start working as soon as we got there. After we'd found a house. Oh I'd so much like to live in a house again!"

Not even careful to limit the yearning in her voice, she'd

actually done a pirouette and let her hands course through her hair, shaking it free of its restraining band. Nothing will happen. We'll agree to this like we've agreed to a thousand other things, why drag a dead marriage three thousand miles west? "Well, I guess I could write Harvey and see what he thinks the chances are, find out who's who in the departments out there, what face I should use to present myself. And records. Oh man, it means applications and transcripts and that whole scene again, letters of recommendation and figuring out what Admissions Committees would like to hear about you. I'm really not up to all that, I've lost touch. Writing up case records is another world." And ruefully, to forestall her thinking that he was writing it off: "I won't be able to see these years as anything but wasted, once I'm back in school."

Finally she was across the room to him, light touch on the back of his neck. "That's crazy. You'll see, you'll see as soon as you get there. They'll all seem like kids next to you. You don't see how much these two years have changed you, but I do."

"Maybe wasted's a silly way to put it," with his hands circling her waist, lightly. "Just clogged, and blocked. Most days I wake up feeling like I've been bled during the night. Some squalid anemia of the soul." I'll forget to write and you won't mention it, first because you're not certain I've really forgotten and then because you're afraid I might've forgotten on purpose. Finally you'll convince yourself that even bringing it up would irritate me too much to risk it. This whole maneuver has bought us maybe a month at our current rate, is that what you bargained for?

174

Afterwards, as she curled into the hollow of his arm and shoulder, he let himself drift, suspended, above his subsiding skin, fresh muscles pulsing. "It's been a long time since it's been anything like that," she said. "Uhhmm," he murmured, bobbing on lazy currents toward his stomach. "How long?" she wondered. He grinned, stray knuckles scraped, half-heartedly chastising, into her hair. "No time to worry about that now, silly. Just be thankful it still happens." Short-circuited a spasm of irritation and drifted down to rejoin the currents on which his head floated. She yawned, moist lips against his chest and wriggled lower, her hair tickled his shoulders. "I'm so sleepy. I stayed awake all night worrying about you. I imagined a hundred places where you were—and who you were with."

The last thing he remembered was fumbling to touch her hair, how long had they slept? Buzzer startled him but he wasn't alarmed, could be anybody. Nothing vestigial warned him to get up, beat her to the door, whatever instincts guided him had suddenly turned traitor. "Whatever it is, we don't want any," he mumbled. "They'll go away." But she was already extracting herself. "I'll go." He opened reluctant eyes to reward himself with the sight of her as she slipped her robe on, she's crazy to worry, those breasts will never go saggy. Decided to stay awake till she came back to bed, might even find her interested again. Or committed enough, anyway, to give it another try. He heard the tumblers snap as she unlocked the door.

Angelina stared at Laurie's sleep-puffed face. "What the hell are you doing home, you're supposed to be away for the whole weekend!" Half turned away, but probably she was too angry. "Look, just tell your goddam husband I want these laundered and I want him to pay for them. And tell him I said he was a pig!" She shouted the last words over her shoulder, already across the landing. Laurie stood in her doorway, her robe falling loose over her shoulders, staring down at the tangle of striped sheets Angelina had bundled into her arms.

SAL *I took him back to the neighborhood for a haircut just before his trial. I didn't bother to ask the Lieutenant for permission, and besides we got a barber from Louie's comes in every week. But I figured he deserves something better than a towel wrapped around him in his own cell, so I took him out, told the boys we were headed cross-town for another set of pictures, nobody asked any questions. And I paid, shave and a full trim. Longo was busy, the new guy he hired to replace Freddie can't keep his mouth shut, keeps humming and singing and asking questions while he's massaging Dutch's neck, wants to know if Dutch wants a little men's scent, the ladies will come crawling like flies. "Just don't talk so much and hurry it up, buddy." Where he's going he won't have trouble keeping the ladies off. Walking across Canal Street I slowed down to wait for him, loosened my collar, this heat turns my pores on and off like taps, I sweat dishwater. He didn't notice anything, didn't bother to look, some stupid idea of mine that he'd appreciate a last stroll through the neighborhood. He walked with his shoulders hunched and his head tucked in, I couldn't even tell if he understood he was never coming back. I didn't bother to put the cuffs on him, we walked shoulder to shoulder right through the neighborhood, I nodded hello to maybe a dozen people who never noticed him. Fresh-shaved cheeks and a part down the middle of his slick-combed hair, I offered to buy him a cannoli and a cup of coffee. "We'll sit outside like we*

176

owned the sidewalk." My big treat fell flat, he couldn't eat the cannoli, just nibbled at it, and he drank the coffee like it was water, two gulps and his cup was empty. "C'mon, Dutch," I said finally, "it's time we were getting back."

Before his stroke leveled him, Geracimo always took him on Saturday mornings, candy-cane pole wreathed in cigar smoke, hair like sawdust shavings littering the tile floor. Three full swing-arounds in a creaking leather-trimmed chair his reward for promising not to squirm beneath thin fingers that pinned starched striped sheets round his neck; he held his breath, straining to see his reflection swaddled in flowing pin-stripes. "That's what you'll look like in prison," Geracimo always chuckled. Snick-snick-snick of the scissors cleansed as they sheared, his neck and ears gradually emerged, unfeathered. The nicest part he closed his eyes for, long-necked bottle with a syrup dispenser snout, blue-water tonic, vinegar and mint, three shakes into his hair and strong hands rubbing till his scalp tingled. At the prison the barber wet his hands under the tap, they cut Matto's hair once a month, according to regulations.

177

a note on the type

The text of this book was set on the Fotosetter in a type face called Biretta—the camera version of Bembo, the well-known monotype face. The original cutting of Bembo was made by Francesco Griffo of Bologna only a few years after Columbus discovered America. It was named for Pietro Bembo, the celebrated Renaissance writer and humanist scholar who was made a cardinal and served as secretary to Pope Leo X. It was in recognition of Pietro Bembo's role as cardinal that the name Biretta was chosen for the film adaptation of the face.

Sturdy, well balanced, and finely proportioned, Bembo is a face of rare beauty. It is, at the same time, extremely legible in all of its sizes.

Composed by Westcott & Thomson, Inc., Philadelphia, Pennsylvania. Printed by Universal Lithographer, Timonium, Maryland. Bound by L. H. Jenkins, Richmond, Virginia.